THE ASSASSIN
THE COMPLETE ADVENTURES OF CORDIE,
SOLDIER OF FORTUNE, VOLUME 6

THE ASSASSIN
THE COMPLETE ADVENTURES OF CORDIE, SOLDIER OF FORTUNE, VOLUME 6

W. WIRT

ILLUSTRATED BY
SAMUEL CAHAN

COVER BY
PAUL STAHR

POPULAR PUBLICATIONS · 2023

TABLE OF CONTENTS

THE ASSASSIN

*If Jimmie Cordie finds in Manchuria a certain
New York gangster hired by the Japs, war
between America and Japan can be averted*

1

SECRET PLANS

COLONEL TAKARA, JAPANESE Military Intelligence, sat at his desk in the building taken over by the M.I. in San-Sing, Manchukuo. The colonel was very well pleased with himself and the world in general as he painstakingly went over a plan that he had spent a good deal of time maturing. If it succeeded, there was no question in the colonel's mind but that war would be declared between the United States of America and Japan and that was what the colonel wanted above all else. He would go over it again, searching for weak spots and then—

The door opened and a young Japanese officer came in. Colonel Takara looked up and pushed aside the pad of paper on which he was scrawling meaningless figures.

"Pardon me for interrupting you, Colonel. I have news that I thought you would like to hear at once."

"You are pardoned, Major Shiga. Sit down. When did you return from the North?"

"I arrived an hour ago. The news is this. The Big Swords are marching towards Khabarovsk, a full division of them. They go to join the dogs of the Soviet who are concentrating there. With them ride Chang-lung Liang and—here is the best part of the news, Colonel. Also with them are the soldiers of fortune that Lieutenant-General Nagayo would give much to have brought before him—living or dead. We can attack them at the—but, Colonel, you do not seem interested?"

"I am interested, of course, Major Shiga. But at the moment, I have another matter on my mind of far greater importance than the slaying of a few Big Swords and the mongrels who lead them. If my—"

"Of greater importance! What could be more so, Colonel? For three years the Big Swords have been a thorn in our sides and the Yankee dogs have flouted us time and again. We cannot bring up many troops to attack, at the moment, but those that are here will follow us to the death.

"We can cut our way in to Chang-lung Liang and the Yankees who ride close to him and slay them before we die. What a glorious death! To die after sending to the lowest hell the curs who have dared snap at the soldiers of Nippon.

Our names will be honored and placed in song and history! What a glorious chance has been given us!"

Colonel Takara listened to the young officer in whose eyes glowed the "spirit of Japan." Major Shiga was all for conquest and glory, a true Japanese militarist. The Colonel watched him through half closed eyes. Takara loved Japan and would die if necessary in her defense, but—the Takara clan came first. He took very good care to hide his feelings and outwardly was, as other officers, all for Nippon at any time.

As he listened to Major Shiga, who went on chanting of glory and honor and the privilege of dying, he was mulling over in his mind the idea of using the young hotspur to further the plan. He knew that Shiga was of the "Samurai" and that the Shiga clan ranked with the highest in Japan. It might be well—in case anything slipped—to have with him one of the Shiga. Not that anything could happen, but—he needed someone. And he decided to try for Shiga.

Jimmie Cordie leading,
the Manchus closed in.

"What you say, Major," he said, smoothly, "is true—all of it. You could not say otherwise, being of the Shiga. It is in your blood as it is in mine.

"I feel as you feel, but—"here the Colonel smiled, "being quite a few years older than you, it may be that words do not come as readily to my lips."

"We will go then? There are two regiments here and a field battery. Also two troops of cavalry. We can make a surprise attack at night on their headquarters. What honor to me if I can kill this Captain Cordie who disfigured Lieutenant-General Nagayo when—"

"You say Captain Cordie of the Big Swords did that? I did not know it. I have been more or less in the South and am not familiar with matters up here."

"Yes, Colonel. Lieutenant-General Nagayo was then Colonel Nagayo. I was a lieutenant. We trapped some of the Big Swords on an island and during the fight that followed Colonel Nagayo closed with Captain Cordie who struck him in the face with the hilt of a sword. That is why I say that Lieutenant-General Nagayo would give much to have—"

"I do not quite understand, Major. You say the Big Swords were trapped on an island? How, then, does it happen that Captain Cordie is still alive and—"

"Why, they—they—through a trick, they escaped us."

Colonel Takara smiled. "I have heard that they were very good at—shall I say, tricks, Major?"

"That is true, Colonel. Pardon me if I say so, but we are wasting valuable time, are we not? I—I would give much to be the one to take this Captain Cordie and those with him. Much? I will cheerfully give my life. What honor would be mine and—"

COLONEL TAKARA HAD no intention of letting Shiga get started off again, so he interrupted, "I know that you would, Major. You think that I am not very enthusiastic about the matter, do you not? That is a mistake, I am. But at the moment, I am planning something in which there is much more glory for those participating than there is in the taking or slaying of Captain Cordie."

If Colonel Takara's plan was a success there is no question but what there would be glory in it for the Japanese Intelligence officers taking part and also—the Takara clan would become much more wealthy.

They were munition makers with large plants and—war with the Soviet looked farther than ever away. War scare after war scare, as far as the United States was concerned, had fizzled out. Nippon had plenty of ammunition on hand to take care of Manchukuo. If war did come with the United States, the Takara clan would become—

It may be that the Japanese colonel was motivated by purely patriotic reasons. To strike at the United States now, before the colossus of the North fully armed itself, was good strategy. That any human being would deliberately plot to involve two nations in bloody war so that munition manufacturers might benefit, is not conceivable. Yet Colonel Takara's face was impassive as he advanced the bait of "glory" to Major Shiga. Even if he had the baser motive, he and Shiga would make a good combination. One out for glory and the other for wealth and power. The Colonel knew better than to mention profits in munition to one of the Shiga clan.

"You are planning something? In which there is more glory? What that is—I beg your pardon, Colonel; I, a mere major, should not ask."

"I do not mind telling you, Major. It may be that I can find a place for you. There will be glory enough for all. First, on your word of honor as a Shiga clansman, if you do not care to join me, you will never divulge, in any way, shape or manner, what I tell you."

"On the word of honor of a Shiga clansman."

"It is this. Two weeks from today, the Emperor Kang Teh, also known as Henry Pu-yi, goes to Shuntien to pray at the Altar of Heaven. As he nears the Altar, he will be fired on from a window. The—"

"Wait. I do not understand. You are telling me now of what will happen two weeks from now? Truly, you must be a—"

"I am nothing but an Intelligence officer, Major, as yourself. If you will let me finish without interruption, matters will be clear to you."

"THE EMPEROR OF Manchukuo will be fired upon by a rifleman and if not instantly killed, will be at least wounded. But he will be shot dead because—I get ahead of my story. As the shot is fired, two Nippon Intelligence officers who are in front of the building run up the stairs and into the room from whose window the shot came. They kill the man who kneels by the window rifle at shoulder. He is—an American."

"I—I—you say that the Emperor is killed? Or wounded? But that—that is—"

"What, compared with the glory and honor of chastising the greatest bluffers in the world, the Yankees?"

"But, he is the Emperor. I am afraid I do not follow you, Colonel Takara."

"A puppet Emperor, only. Nippon can choose among fifty for another puppet.

"What is his life if the losing of it will give us the longed for chance to demonstrate to the bully of the world that he cannot insult Nippon with impunity?"

"Nothing, Colonel. But still I do not follow you."

"If the Emperor of Manchukuo is assassinated by an American—what will all Nippon demand?"

Major Shiga's eyes shone as he answered, "War! War to the death! We will take the Philippines and Hawaiian Islands and then—then we will march through their States, one after the other."

"No question, Major. If we can put the affair through without a slip, we will be the most honored officers in Nippon and—"

"You say if we put the affair through? You mean by that?"

"You are not a child, Major. Surely you understand all of what I am saying to you."

"You mean that we do what the Yankees call—call— what is it? I heard it often when I was over there. I think it is—"

"You are thinking of their expression 'frame up' or 'to frame,' Major."

"That is it. You mean that we manufacture—er— frame—the entire thing?"

"Yes, that is exactly what I mean."

"But—the slaying of Henry Pu-Yi?"

"Do you count him against honor and glory?" asked

Takara, smoothly. "If you do, I will select some other officer. What is he, after all, but a Manchu?"

"You know that I count nothing against the glory of
Nippon. Tell me again of the plan. I—you said that an
American will fire the shot. I did not know there was an
American anywhere near Hsingking or—"

"There is—and I have him. He will fire the shot, Major."

"Knowing that we will kill him right afterwards and—I
see you smile, Colonel. Truly, this is all new to me and you
must be patient."

"I was not smiling at what you said, Major. I was smiling
at a mental picture I had just then of their glorious fleet
sailing to hunt for the Yankee mongrels."

"And I see us burning their White House as the English
did in the War of 1812. They are not prepared and we—this
American? Will he kill Henry Pu-Yi, knowing what will
happen to his country afterwards? What kind of a dog is
he? I thought that all Americans were as we are, ready to
die for—"

"Come and see this man with me. There are many kinds
of Americans, Major. Some of them are not true patriots
like us. We will soon teach them differently."

2

SOVIET ALLIANCE

A BIG SWORD division lay encamped north of the railroad near Khabarovsk. It had come from the Thian Shan range in western Manchukuo, led by the Manchu noble Chang-lung Liang, for whom all Big Swords fought.

Chang had been invited to Khabarovsk by the Soviet commanders to "talk matters over." The Soviet, in case of war with Japan, wanted Chang-lung Liang to ally himself with the Soviet and help protect the railroad and the Siberian border.

The proud old Manchu, who had organized the Big Swords and who had been fighting the Japanese for every foot of territory in northwestern Manchukuo they tried for, was not very keen for the alliance.

He did not like the Soviet and what it stood for, but he disliked the "little men of Nippon" more. He knew that sooner or later the Japs would wipe out the Big Swords and so he thought it over.

"I do not know, Captain Cordie. To league the House of Chi with the Red mongrels means that a stain will be put on the shining honor shield of the House of Chi. The chieftains on High would cover their faces with their robes to hide the scorn in the eyes of the chieftains of the House of Nurhachu and the House of Sinkiang. And yet—if I do not—soon the little men of Nippon will triumph and walled cities in the hills will fall. Men, women and children will be slain or driven out in the cold to freeze and starve. With the help of the Soviet, it may be that the little men can be driven back to their islands and—speak plainly your thoughts to me, O you who take the place of the son denied me by the Gods."

The slim, wiry, blackeyed American, second in command of the Big Swords, smiled as he answered, "I cannot think as you think, Lord Chang. I can think only as a soldier of fortune thinks. You are a Manchu noble, Head of the House of Chi. I am James Cordie, an American who fights for pay. I know nothing of—"

"It is true that you are an American soldier of fortune and also true that you fight for pay and yet—your spirit is that of a chieftain. You would fight at my side without pay, Captain Cordie?"

"Yes."

"Know that I, Chang-lung Liang, Head of the House of Chi, say that in all things you are my equal. Now, tell me your thoughts."

Jimmie Cordie, fighter in the far places for war lord or potentate, really liked and highly respected the grim, dour, old Manchu fighter. "All right, here they are. The chieftains on High surely will know why you league the House of Chi with the Soviet. Instead of thinking a stain has been put on the shining honor shield they will smile and hold their heads proudly, knowing that you are but playing a Manchu trick on both the Reds and the little men of Nippon.

"The Big Swords are at war with the little men, and if the

Soviet wish to make love to the Big Swords—why not let them think that their love is acceptable? The chieftains know that the Big Swords make war to protect the men and women and little ones. They will also know why the House of Chi permits love making. What I am trying to say is, Chang,

Jimmie Cordie

that according to your belief, the chieftains sit on High and look down on their descendants. Well, if they do that—they know what makes their descendants do things. That is about as clear as mud, but it's the best I can do."

"I understand, Captain Cordie. It is not, as you say, mud. It is a fresh, clean wind that has driven the fog from my brain. I comprehend what you are saying."

"From what I know of you, resplendent Head of the House of Chi, I do not think there was ever very much fog around your brain," Jimmie answered, with a grin. "The way I look at it is this. Sooner or later we are due for cleaning—I mean we will be wiped out."

"Many of the foul spirits that now inhabit the bodies of the little curs will have winged their way to the lowest hell before that happens, Captain Cordie."

"NO QUESTION ABOUT that. If it were man to man, or even ten to one, I would say that the Big Swords play a lone hand, withdrawing to the hills. But it isn't Chang. The Japs have only been fooling around with us. A division here and a division there. Sooner or later they will get our scalp.

"If we throw in with the Soviet we are not any worse off than we were before and if the Soviet wins, which I think it will, we can dicker with them for a certain territory to be held by the Big Swords, independently. If the Soviet gets licked, we can still fuss around with Mister Jap. Here is what I think will happen.

"The Soviet air force will knock the principal cities of Japan into cocked hats right after war has been declared. If that is the case, all Japs here in Manchukuo will be left right up in the air. And then, maybe the Chinese and the Big Swords can make them execute one of their famous retreating movements towards the sea."

"You have once more put the House of Chi in your debt, Captain Cordie. I think now as you think. Will you do an old man the honor of dining with him to-night? Afterwards I will explain the matter to the nobles of the House of Chi."

"I will be glad to, Lord Chang. I ride now to inspect the outposts and the guard."

As Jimmie left the headquarters tent, a big, burly, redheaded man detached himself from a group of Manchu officers and joined Jimmie.

"What the hell kept ye, ye scut ave the world?" he demanded. " 'Tis an hour I have been waitin' for ye."

"Yeah? Why didn't you send in word you were waiting, Mr. Dolan? Chang and I would have been glad to break up our conference if we had known that—"

"Says ye, that's all. Jimmie, what did the old bird want with ye?"

"Quit talking so disrespectfully of the Marshal Chang-lung Liang, you redheaded ape, I'm s'prised at you, Mr. Dolan."

"Ye are like hell. I was sittin' in a game with that misbegotten Yid and the Boston Bean and the both ave them was cheatin' so I cashed in the while I was ahead. Some day I'll—"

Grigsby

"I'll bet you will. Want to take a ride? I'm going around the outposts for a little look see."

"Sure I'll go wid ye, Jimmie," That answer did not surprise Jimmie any. From the day that Red Dolan first met Jimmie Cordie in the Foreign Legion, Red had stuck as close to Jimmie as possible. Whatever Jimmie did was the thing to do. Whatever Jimmie said was the thing to say, as far as Red went.

"What did he want?" Red asked again as they walked along.

"For Pete's sake! What do you care? If you must know he was deciding whether to throw in with the Soviet or not. Now you know all about it."

"I do not. What did ye tell him to do?"

"What did I tell Chang-lung Liang to do? Sure you're the King of the Cannibal Islands. Don't let that bad old Yid kid you different. Go back and tell him I said that—"

"Aw, go to hell, ye black muzzled shrimp. If ye was half the size ave a real man 'tis me that would be takin' ye apart long before now."

Jimmie laughed, "Lucky for me I'm little. Get your horse, Red. I'll tell you all about it as we go along."

THE BIG SWORDS, although in friendly territory, kept ward and watch as they did in the hills. Jimmie Cordie found the outposts and far flung patrols alert and where they ought to be. He and Red, who was, with two other soldiers of fortune, in command of the machine and rapid fire guns, rode finally up to the last outpost to be visited. The Manchu officer and the men of the outpost greeted the two Americans with punctilious salutes and then, smiles. All of the Big Swords, Manchus, Chinese, Tartars, Mongols, Cossacks, and Afghans, as well as the men of twenty different hill tribes, paid full tribute to the fighting ability of the adventurers who led them, and respected them for their fair, even justice.

"Hullo, Hsai," Jimmie said, in Pushtu, the universal language of the border. "Everything appears to be quiet along the Potomac."

"Yes, everything is quiet, honorable elder brother," answered the Manchu, "I do not know where the Potomac is but—"

Two riders of one of the patrols came up. With them rode a girl. She was not dressed for riding but she sat her horse as if she had ridden before. Jimmie and Red, in the bright moonlight, could see that she was white and either American or English.

"This woman," one of the riders said to the Manchu, "was with two Chinese when we met them. Wong Lu, who commands the patrol, sent us with her to you. She asks for Lord Grigsby."

The girl had been looking at Jimmie and Red. "Oh! I know that I am all right now. I am hunting for George Grigsby, who is an officer of the Big Swords. Do you know him?"

Red Dolan

"Very well indeed," Jimmie Cordie answered with a smile, "I am Captain Cordie and this is Captain Dolan. Major Grigsby is—"

"Captain Cordie! You—you are Jimmie Cordie?"

"That's right, I'm Jimmie Cordie and this is the justly famous Red Dolan, better known as—"

"Enough," interrupted Red. "Do ye not see that she is all in, ye blind half pint ave nawthin? Never mind him, alanna. If the world was fallin' in he'd have to joke. George Grigsby is the buddy av us, darlin', and 'tis us that will take ye to him at wance."

"I—I am not—not all in but I haven't eaten since last night and I have—come—I reckon it is the—relief of—" she swayed in the saddle.

Both Jimmie and Red spurred their horses forward to catch her, Red beating Jimmie to it. He reached out a brawny arm and lifted the girl from her horse as easily as a woman lifts a baby. Red Dolan was all of two hundred and thirty pounds and none of it fat. The girl was not over five feet four inches and would not go over a hundred and ten pounds. Red held her in the crook of his arm and glared at Jimmie Cordie. Mr. Dolan would fight any odds, anywhere and at any place and really enjoy himself while doing it. But any woman or child could twist the big fighting man around a little finger without half trying.

"Get something to eat, ye dish faced monkey," he commanded Hsai, "and something to drink and make it snappy. What the hell are ye standin' there for?" It may have been lucky for Mr. Dolan that he spoke in English which the Manchu noble did not understand.

Jimmie translated the part of Red's command concerning food and drink and Hsai ran towards the outpost's food supply.

"No," the girl said, "I—I have not fainted. I—I—put me down, Captain Dolan."

Jimmie dismounted and Red eased the girl into Jimmie's arms. "Easy now, darlin'. Jimmie will have ye on the little feet ave ye widout ye jumpin'."

Jimmie Cordie laughed as he stood the girl on her feet. "Once Mr. Dolan takes charge of anyone, there is no use of—"

"Oh, if you only knew how glad I am that—that someone is ready to take charge of me. I have been so long away from my kind of men-folks that—that—please, never mind about any food. I must get to George Grigsby at once. Something awful is going to happen and it may be too late even now to stop—" she fainted.

"This is a real one, Red. What have you got there, Hsai? Brandy? Open it up. Turn her a little, Red. Get some cold water, Hsai. That's all it is, Red. She is breathing. Have some hot soup made ready, Hsai. She'll be all right in a minute or two."

"Jimmie, does she mean that something is going to happen to George?"

"How do I know? I'm no mind reader. Hold her chin up a little. And what a Yank girl is doing here beyond Khabarovsk, I don't know either."

3

A NEW YORK KILLER

LOUIS WALTER CHAPMAN, born of decent, hardworking, God fearing New England parents, thirty-four years old, at one time ace killer of Angy Wenzler's mob in New York, lay on a cot in a room above a Chinese shop in San-sing. He had gone the route since he was fifteen. Gay cat, lush toucher, petty larceny thief, bootlegger, and at last—a killer. But now, his once clever, alert brain was deadened by drugs and hardly functioned at all.

Time was when he would have listened to what a Japanese officer proposed, agreed to it, taken money in advance and then double crossed the Japanese, laughing as he did so. But that day was well past for "Louie" Chapman of the Wenzler gang. Now all he thought of was getting enough of the drug to make him feel well and happy. "It's about time you got here," he snarled, raising himself up on an elbow as Colonel Takara entered with Major Shiga. "Have you brought me the stuff?"

Colonel Takara handed Chapman a little box and the two Japanese officers watched him open it with trembling fingers. They watched him pour some of the powder on the back of his right hand and then sniff the powder. Their faces and eyes were impassive but in their hearts there was utter contempt for this American.

"That's better," Chapman said, after a moment or so. "Who is this guy with you?"

"This guy," Colonel Takara answered in perfect English, "is named Shiga. He is with me in this matter, Mr. Chapman. I brought him here so that he might see and talk to you. I think he wishes to be convinced that you are ready and willing to do as you have agreed to do."

"Yeah? Well, how many times must I tell you that for five grand I'd take all the Chinks in China for a ride?"

"A grand?" asked Major Shiga, puzzled. He also spoke English and understood it but not as well as Colonel Takara. "And 'take for a ride'? Also, he speaks of Chinks. I do not understand."

CHAPMAN LAUGHED. THE drug was working now. "Your buddy isn't wise like you, is he? Listen, punk. A grand is one thousand dollars. Five grand, five thousand dollars. Take for a ride means to kill, see? And a Chink is—what the hell is confusing about that? A Chink is a Chink."

"Mr. Chapman," Colonel Takara said, smoothly, "does not differentiate between a Manchu and a Chinese, Major."

"Whatever that is," sneered Chapman. "Well—so what?"

"As I have said, I brought this gentleman here so that he might—"

"I heard you the first time. O.K., feller. I will rub out any louse, anytime, for five grand. All you got to do is to show him to me and have the coin ready."

"You mean that you will kill anyone, no matter who he is?" asked Major Shiga, honestly amazed.

"What the hell do I care who he is. That isn't my business. My business is to cool him off. What the hell is this, a meeting of the Sunday school class?"

"Not at all, Mr. Chapman. It is only that I wanted—"

"Yeah? Well, he's done it. Listen, I get five grand and get put on a boat for London for killing this guy for you, Pu-yi, don't I? All right. Put me where I can see him and give me a rod or a rifle. That's all there is to it. I'm ready any time. You keep me in shape with the stuff and I'll do the rest."

"Are you sure you can hit the guy?" asked Major Shiga. "Your nerves do not seem to be in very good condition, Mr. Chapman."

"Yeah? Well—listen, punk. I can take a rod or a rifle or a Tommy-gun and knock 'em off the Christmas tree just as far as I can see 'em. What do you know about that? Once in Detroit when I was working for the Purples, I—" he told a long rambling story about the killing of four rival gangsters. The two dapper little Japanese officers listened gravely and at the finish, sucked their breath in to show admiration.

"That's the kind of a lad I am. You get everything set and I'll do the rest. Scram out of here, will you? I want to hit the hay."

Once on the street, Major Shiga shook his head, "I did not know that there were men such as he. He is like a viper, Colonel. That is it, he is a human snake."

"There are many such as he in America. They are called killers. You evidently did not meet any of them while you were there."

"Do you think he really believes that you—that we will arrange his safe departure on a ship after he has assassinated the Emperor of Manchukuo?"

"The drug has weakened his brain, Major. He does not reason things out now—if he ever did. He has killed for money before and been protected afterwards and so—he thinks he will be protected now."

"That is probably correct. I have just thought of something. This Chinese shop-

Fighting Yid

keeper—he knows that you, and now I, have been with this killer."

"That is right. Do you know who this shopkeeper is?"

"No—not any more than his name is T'ang Li, a Chinese."

HE IS A spy for Nippon and his family all live on my father's estate in Himeji. He knows what would happen to them as well as to himself if he talked concerning one of the Takara. And what could he tell if he did talk? That he had seen Colonel Takara talking to the American who assassinated Henry Pu-Yi before the deed? And that I had with me another Japanese officer? If he told that, of which there is not the slightest chance, I would readily admit it. I wished to find out why he was in Manchukuo. He explained that he was a writer about to begin a book about the Manchus. Had I thought for an instant that he was anything else I would have had him sent from the coun-

try. You would say the
same."

"And when you first
contacted him?"

"In Vladivostok. I was
not then Colonel Takara
of the Japanese Intelli-
gence, I assure you."

"What were you?"
asked Major Shiga with
a smile. "I have heard
that you are more than
clever disguising your-
self."

Carewe

"I was a Merkits tribesman. Many men have met and
talked to this Yankee killer, Major. Because I have and you
have, does that mean that we arranged an assassination?
What proof could possibly be brought forth? He will be
taken to the proper place under cover and once there—his
body will be taken from there. Can a dead body talk?"

"No. How did he get here?"

"In a wagon, drugged and covered with a canvas. I have
been very, very careful, Major, in this affair. If you will come
with me to my quarters I will go into details."

"I will be glad to, Colonel. I have thought of something
else. While we are waiting, why can we not go after the Big
Swords officers who have laughed and tricked—"

"You evidently have them on the brain. In trying for
them we very possibly might be removed from this earth.
Forget the lesser for the greater."

"You are right, Colonel."

4

COUNTER-PLANS

A GIRL ENTERED the tent, followed by Jimmie Cordie and Red Dolan. Jimmie had been right when he said, "she'll be all right in a minute or two." The brandy and the hot, thick soup had given the girl new strength. After ten minutes' rest, they had ridden with her to the Big Sword division.

As she came in, the four soldiers of fortune rose from their seats. Carewe, to whom Grigsby had been trying to explain something connected with artillery fire, was slim and boyish looking, with clean cut delicate features. A young Englishman and a fighter from the top of his head to the tips of his toes. The Yid was about as broad as he was long and looked fat. There was no fat on him, he was all bone and muscle. Grigsby, broad shouldered, lean, with Indian face, was fully as big as Red Dolan although he did not look it.

One thing they all had in common and that was cool, calm eyes. Another thing was tight lips and the ease of their movements showed perfect coordination between brain and muscles. The tent was well lighted with several big, fat candles. The girl looked at them, one after the other, until she got to Grigsby, then she took a step forward, smiling a little. "I reckon you're George Grigsby?"

"That's right," Grigsby answered, stepping up to her, "I'm George Grigsby, honey. Who might you be? Wait a minute until I get me a right good look at you. Shucks, you're a Shelby."

Jimmie Cordie smiled inwardly as he heard Grigsby drop right into the slow, drawling "hill" talk.

"That's right. I'm Betty Ann Shelby. That is—I—I was Betty Ann Shelby. I reckon your ma was my aunt Mary Lou."

"Yes suh, my ma was Mary Lou Shelby. We're sure kin, darlin'. Come and sit down and rest. You look right puny. I'll get you something to drink and eat right away and then you—"

"I've had something. I reckon I better tell you right away how I—"

"Take your time, honeychile. You've done reached your kin." He turned to Jimmie Cordie, "May I ask you gentlemen to excuse us for a little while? It may be that my cousin has something to tell me that—"

Betty Ann, who had sat down, rose. "No, George, they need not go. I heard about Captain Cordie and you'all in Vladivostok and I reckon that all the menfolks here are part of what is called Jimmie Cordie's outfit? If they are they can stay."

"Yes, Betty Ann, we are all of Jimmie Cordie's outfit. I reckon Jimmie and Red have already introduced themselves. Allow me to present to you Captain John Cabot Winthrop, called the Boston Bean. The next gentleman to him is Captain Abraham Cohen, called The Fighting Yid. The gentleman beside the table is Captain John Cecil

Carewe. Gentlemen, Miss Elizabeth Ann Shelby, a kins-woman of mine, from the good state of Kentucky."

Jimmie Cordie had smiled again as he heard Grigsby once more become formal in speech, but the smile was wiped out as he saw the girl draw a long breath and her pretty face whiten.

"No, George," she said, "I am no longer Miss Eliza-beth Ann Shelby. I am Mrs. Louise Walter Chapman. I—gentlemen, I reckon I feel right honored to meet you'all but right now I— George, it is about my—my husband that I want to tell you."

"Relax, darlin'. You are all right. Sit down again. Don't you want a little drink before you start telling us? And can't it wait until after you have rested?"

"I reckon I would like a little drink. No, I can't rest until I have told you. I don't know how much time there is left."

After she had the drink, she began, "Four years ago I decided that I'd quit teachin' school down in Kentucky, and go to New York and try to get on the stage, dancin'. So I saved my money and—"

IT WAS A long story Betty Ann told. It summed up to this. She went to New York and after taking some danc-ing lessons, became a member of the chorus of a musical comedy. She met a man she thought was a broker and after six months, married him. His name was Louis Walter Chapman. He furnished a luxurious apartment and for a year they were happy. Later she found out that instead of being a broker, he was a gangster—a killer of the Angy Wenzler mob. She asked him about it and he admitted it. He began drinking heavily—sank lower and lower—she stuck to him because in her Kentucky code he was "her man." At last, Angy Wenzler told him to leave town or get rubbed out. A man she knew got him the job of bodyguard to a young multimillionaire who was going around the world.

The young man had no objection to her going along as a stewardess. She went, hoping that the sea voyage would straighten Chapman out. It did not. Every port the yacht touched Chapman got drunk and at last began using drugs. At Vladivostok the multimillionaire discharged him. They went on shore and she got a job in One Eyed Jack's saloon as dancing girl. Chapman, she thought, was getting feeble-minded. When he was sober, which became more and more seldom, he was not so bad but when drunk or under the influence of drugs—not so good for her. He had killed whatever love she had for him but still he was her man and she stuck. One night he came to the squalid room they were existing in, and boasted that soon he was going to have plenty of money and they would go to England.

"I asked him how he was going to get the money and he laughed at me. Finally he said he was going to spot—I reckon that was the word—someone named Pu-yi. He said that he'd make cold pie out of Pu-yi."

Jimmie Cordie had not been paying much attention, having had a hard day and being both tired and sleepy. He thought that Betty Ann was telling a hard luck story of married life and that it would end by Grigsby seeing to it that she arrived home in Kentucky. But when she said "spot" and "Pu-yi," Jimmie literally sat up and took notice.

"He said that he was going to spot someone named Pu-yi?" he asked.

"Yes, Captain Cordie. I begged him not to do it but he

just kept on laughing and said for me to stay right in Vladivostok until he got back. That he'd have the money and we'd go to England."

"Do you know whether or not he was friendly with any Russians or Japanese or Chinese in Vladivostok?"

"Jimmie, what are ye drivin' at?" Red demanded. "She is all in and there ye sit asking questions."

"I guess that is right, Red. If you had rather rest first, Mrs. Chapman, the questions can wait."

"I WISH YOU all would please call me Betty Ann. I am all right, thank you just the same, Captain Dolan."

"Red, darlin'. Never mind that captain stuff wid us. That scut is the Yid and that wan is the Bean and that wan is Carewe and—"

"Betty Ann has already been introduced, you big ape. I will be glad if you call me Jimmie—Betty Ann. Now, did he pal around with any Chinese or Russians or Japanese?"

"Why, I never saw him with any, Jimmie. But the night he left, right after, I went to the place I work and one of the girls came up to me. She said that she wanted to know if my husband knew that the Merk—the some kind of a tribesman—he was meeting was Colonel Takara of the Japanese Military Intelligence."

"Takara? Holy cats! Go ahead, Betty Ann, what did you say?"

"Why, I said I didn't even know he was meeting anyone. She didn't believe it at first and she tried to scare me, I reckon. She said I had better tell what I knew and right away. That One Eyed Jack was for the Soviet all the way through and that he'd make me tell. I reckon she saw that she couldn't scare me and at last, she said that she was convinced that I was tellin' the truth. She asked me to try and find out what they were talkin' about and I told her that my husband had left the city and I didn't know where he was. She said that she'd find out if the—I think it was Mer—Merkids or something like that—the Merkids tribesman had also left the city. Then she left me."

"What was she, Betty Ann?"

"She was a Russian girl, named Sonia Radischev."

"Well, that explains that part of it, anyway. They make a fine pair to draw to, she and—"

"Colonel Takara is one of the fastest Jap agents and Sonia Radischev is just as fast for the Soviet. Don't ask me how I know it, either. It is clear enough up to date. Takara was in Vladivostok disguised as a Merkits tribesman. Sonia Radischev recognized him, no doubt having played against him before. Colonel Takara picked Chapman up and has hired him to kill someone called Pu-yi."

"What happened after Sonia Radischev left you, Betty Ann?"

"THERE WERE TWO men there and they were right drunk. They were talking about the Big Swords and I heard them. They talked about you'all. They said that you'all were up near Khabarovsk. I asked them if the man named Grigsby was George Grigsby from Breathitt County, Kentucky, but they said that his name was George Grigsby and that he was from Kentucky, but they didn't know about the Breathitt County part. They said they were Yanks from Vermont, themselves. I don't know their names."

"It doesn't matter, Betty Ann. And then you decided to come up and find if the George Grigsby was your kinsman, is that it?"

"Yes, suh. I knew that if he were, he'd help me. I reckon that my husband was getting into right bad trouble and that I through George might find him and stop him from spottin' that Pu-yi."

"How long ago was all this?" Jimmie asked.

"Why—it took me three days to get up here and—five days altogether."

"And he gave you no line on where he was going?"

"No, Jimmie. George, do you reckon you can find him?"

"I don't know, honey. Manchukuo is a right big place to start huntin' a man when you don't know where to look. And there are a lot of people south of the railroad who might object to our ramblin' around. We'll do the best we can, Betty Ann."

"I know that you will. My gracious, I can hardly hold my eyes open. Telling you about it is such a relief. I reckon I'm right sleepy."

"You can have my tent, darlin'. There are plenty of blankets on that cot. You roll up in them and go to sleep like a good girl. Don't worry about anything, honeychile. You're a smart girl and we are here to protect you."

"I won't. I mean, I won't worry. I'm glad I made—it—to—" She was sound asleep in her chair. Grigsby picked her up in his arms and carried her to the cot and tucked her up in soft blankets. Then the soldiers of fortune tiptoed out of the tent and sat down a little ways from it on the ground.

"Let's get down to cases," Grigsby drawled, "let's figure it out, Jimmie."

"When Betty Ann mentioned Pu-yi, I got a flash from the good Lord knows where that it was Henry Pu-yi.

Let's say that a Japanese Intelligence officer has framed an American killer to kill the Emperor of Manchukuo."

"And what the hell would he do that for?" demanded Red. "Didn't the little pink-toed banties put the scut as Emperor?"

"They did, Mr. Dolan. That's why my hunch won't jell. Why a Jap Intelligence officer, of all men, would frame to have Henry Pu-Yi ascend on High, after the Japs—it doesn't make sense. Maybeso my poor old brain is failing. And it is no wonder after years of associating with morons like—"

JIMMIE CORDIE BEGAN to whistle softly. The soldiers of fortune sat absolutely still. Jimmie had a habit of whistling some old hymn and right afterwards advance some plan or explanation. This time he reached "you may rescue—you—may save."

"Well—this is wilder than nine hundred dollars but maybeso could be. The Jap Intelligence want war with Uncle Sam. Most of the military do. They would give their eye teeth to get something that would make all the Japs back home rear up on their hind legs and yell for battle. What could be sweeter than to have an American assassinate Henry Pu-Yi and get caught in the act? It would be 'up and at 'em' from all Japs over five years old. Japan would declare war inside of twenty-four hours and—"

"Wait a minute, Jimmie. There is a flaw in your 'what could be sweeter,' old kid," Grigsby said. "You say that the American killer gets caught in the act. Do you think that the Japs can pay enough to a killer to get caught in the act of killing the Emperor of Manchukuo? He surely must know what would happen to him right afterwards. If he has any brains at all, he knows that he would be torn apart."

"That's right, George. And yet—"

"Vate. Maybeso de Japs have told it to him dot he vill be protected. Didn't Betty Ann say dot she thought he vos gettink feeble-minded?"

"Yid, I think you have nicked it. Let's go on the assumption that he has been promised protection and not knowing Misto Jap, believes he will get it. Here it is, then. The Jap M.I. have framed an American killer to assassinate Henry Pu-Yi. Why—to catch him right after the act and proclaim to the world that Uncle Sam sic'd him on. Why should they do that? Because they know that all Japan would demand war with the United States and that is what they want. There is your motive, Bean.

"How does that sound to you, George?"

"O.K."

"To you, Carewe?"

"Quite so, Jimmie."

"To you, Bean?"

"Yes, Jeems."

"To you, Yid?"

"Oi, vot a kvestion?"

"I don't have to ask you, Red. We'll accept it as the layout. Now, what to do?"

"Dot's easy. Dey have taken it de killer to vare Henry Pu-Yi is. Und vare is dot you ask, Irisher? Poppa vill tell it you. Dey have taken him to San-sing or maybeso so right smack into Shuntien vich is vare de Altar is. San-sing is only—"

"Who the hell asked ye a question, ye benighted Yid monkey? What are ye buttin' in for? We know where—"

"There is only one thing I can see to do and that is go in and get this American killer before he starts something that will take a few million men to finish. I will take Carewe and get down to Shuntien. There are probably some friends of mine around there who will give me a hand if—"

"WHAT! YE WILL take this little rooster ave the North wid ye? Ye will like hell, Jimmie Cordie! I go wid ye, ye shrimp."

"For Pete's sake, let's not start that. You can't go, Red. The Jap troops around there are of the Seventh division and they know that red topknot of yours full well. I—"

"And they don't know that mug ave yours at all, is that it? For wan that knows me, there is ten that know ye. Who led the charge agin the bamalam midgets at Fu-chung, answer me that?"

"Not so good, Jimmie," Grigsby said. "Red is right. We are all known to more than a few officers and men of the Seventh division. Don't forget they are clever and—"

"Vate. I got it. Listen. I go it in und I say to dem, 'I am tired of foolink around mit de Big Swords who are a bunch of bums, especially de redhead Irish loafaire und de guy dot eats it beans all de time. I—'"

"Cut that stuff out, Yid," Jimmie ordered. "Get down to cases."

"I am down to cases, Jimmie. I say dot if dey vill pay me two thousand smackers I vill bring it in de Bean und Red Dolan mit handcuffs on dem. Den, ven ve get it inside de lines, Red und de Bean escape from me. Ve find it dis killiare und ve do a little killink ourselves. Den ve head for home sveet home. Vot could be sveeter?"

"A whole hell ave a lot ave things, ye Yid polecat," began Red, hotly.

"So—ye are to bring us in wid cuffs on, are ye? Ye, a Cohen, bring in a Dolan with cuffs on?"

"Argue it out with the Yid later. It wouldn't stick, Yid. The Japs know you from old. All you'd get is the Bronx cheer and the end of a rope. They know darn well that none of us would sell the others out."

"Supposing we were all brought in, Jeems?" asked the Boston Bean.

The Big Swords officers all stared at the bored, sleepy looking gentleman who had been born in Boston Massachusetts. In the Orient, whenever soldiers of fortune were gathering forces to go anywhere after anything, someone would say: "Let's get the Codfish Duke of Massachusetts to go along." The Bean's sleepy, sorrowful look was very misleading. He was never sorrowful and the sleepy look would vanish in a split second when there was need of action.

"All right," Jimmie said. "Let's suppose we are all brought in. Go on from there, if it won't be too much effort, Brown Bread." The Bean was called anything that even remotely suggested his birthplace.

"It will be an effort, Jeems," the Bean sighed mournfully, "but I will, as ever, sacrifice myself for the cause." This brought a disdainful snort from Mr. Dolan, but the Bean ignored it. "What was the name of that general in the Spanish-American war? The one who pulled a fast one an Aguinaldo?"

"You mean Funston?"

"That's him, Jeems. Go find someone to bring us in, me good man. After you have done 'er—come back and wake me up. Adios, amigo Red, I go to ze so lofly land of ze sweet dreams and—"

"Holy cats! Stay awake Codfish or I will permit Red to go to work on you. George, didn't that Soviet officer we were talking to the other day say something about the Badakshan tribesmen throwing in with the Japs?"

"HE SAID THAT they were marching south of the railroad towards Hsin King. The Soviet patrols had seen them near the Hue river."

"That's right. I remember now. He asked us if we thought that Chang-lung Liang would stop them with the Big Swords. If old Mangali Boga is still their Khan and along with them, maybeso can do."

"Do what? Tell us, ye black muzzled scut?"

"Wait until I see Chang. While I am gone, George, or you, Codfish, instruct the class about how General Funston fooled Aguinaldo during de wah wid Spain ov'ah in de Fullaprune Islands."

"Have ye gone nuts?" Red asked.

"Sure, heap plenty nuts, leadhead," Jimmie answered as he started for Chang's quarters.

In about a half an hour he came back. "All set, gents. Chang says that we can have a furlough and that all the treasure of the House of Chi is mine to do with as I wish. Speak respectfully to a billionaire, youse guys. We ride to see old Mangali Boga. And when I say we I mean all present that desire to go to a party that the Lord knows when we will get home from—if ever."

"Hold it a minute, Jimmie," Grigsby said, as he rose. I have got to make arrangements about Betty Ann so that she is safe and comfortable."

The arrangements Grigsby made put Betty Ann under the wing of Chang-lung Liang, Manchu noble and leader of the Big Swords. And she could not have been put under a safer wing. Chang said that if anything happened to Grigsby he, Chang, would see to it that Mrs. Chapman was "escorted with honor to her home in Kentucky." Betty Ann was awakened and told that they were going after her husband and that she was to be a good girl and wait right where she was until they got back with him.

And then, the six soldiers of fortune with one hundred Big Swords, in case any roving bandits were met, rode for the Badakshan tribesmen.

5

STAMPEDE

MAJOR SHIGA WAS young, and he was more or less of a dreamer, craving action all the time. The fact that he was so near glory and had to wait for it to come irked him. Colonel Takara saw it and suggested that he, Shiga, put in his time with one of the cavalry squadrons who were out in the field conducting maneuvers. The squadron kept fairly close to San-sing and the Colonel knew it would be a day or so before the ceremony of Henry Pu-Yi praying at the Altar.

Major Shiga, who knew and liked the officers of the squadron, was only too glad to go. And Colonel Takara was equally glad to have him go.

The major in command was telling Shiga some gossip heard about one of the General Staff, the troops riding at ease behind them. It was almost noon and the outfit was heading for a little creek where they could water the horses.

Two of the advance guard came out of a little stand of timber. Between their horses was a Chinese. The two troopers each had hold of a wrist and as they spurred their horses into a run, the Chinese looked to be taking gigantic leaps forward. It was a cruel, unnecessary thing to do but both the majors laughed as if it were a good joke to see a man's arms almost pulled from the sockets.

Major Yura, the squadron commander, raised his right arm and waved the troopers to him. They came up on the gallop and as they pulled their horses to a plunging halt, let the Chinese go. He fell to the ground. The troopers dismounted and jerked him roughly to his feet.

"If the Major please, the right flank forwards met this Chinese who said he was looking for a Nippon detachment. Lieutenant Aritoma sent us in with—"

"Silence," the major rasped, barely returning the troopers' salute.

"Who are you, pariah cur?" to the Chinese, in Chinese.

The Chinese gasped out his story. About ten miles away, marching to the west, was a Big Swords column of a hundred swords and with them rode six foreign devils who are high officers of all Big Swords.

HE WAS ASKED how he knew they were Big Swords and answered that once, a year ago, he had served at the main encampment of the Big Swords as a servant to one of the Manchu officers.

"Ask him to describe the foreign devils," Major Shiga said. He did not speak very good Chinese although he understood it as do most Jap officers. His eyes were shining as he made the request.

The Chinese described the soldiers of fortune with the detail for which the Chinese are noted.

"It is Captain Cordie and others! What luck! What simon-pure luck! You know who they are, Major?"

"Very well, indeed," answered Major Yura, grimly. "I have met them all several times—for a few moments. It may be that the time has come to repay them for what they did to my command in the mountain pass of the Tien

Shan. Allow me to continue to question this Chinese for a few moments. It may be a trap."

The Chinese told of how he was coming across country and saw the Big Swords and how he sneaked up on them as close as he dared to get a better look. He did not like Big Swords—he was all for Nippon—he had received Nippon gold before for information and so—had run to find any men of Nippon—hoping that he would be rewarded.

At last, Major Yura was convinced that it was not a trap and that it was, as Major Shiga said, "simon-pure luck." Here was a squadron, five hundred strong men, of Nippon cavalry—and ten miles away were a hundred swordsmen and the Americans who were as a thorn in the side of the Japanese. Truly, it was luck.

"You will be rewarded," he promised, then snarled to the troopers: "Take him to Captain Yasamara. My orders are that he is to be well treated and guarded." The Japanese policy is to treat well and heavily reward any Chinese who are of service. The idea being that it will encourage other Chinese to do likewise.

As the troopers rode away, the Chinese now walking easily between them, Major Yura said, with a tight lipped smile, "We will see what we can do for the one hundred Big Swords and the Yankee adventurers who think that they alone are clever."

Three hours later, the squadron dismounted, the horses, save those of one troop, in a blind canyon to the left lay in ambush across the path of the Big Swords. Scouts had been sent out and the column located, the direction of the march ascertained, scouts left to report any change and the ambush arranged. One troop was concealed to the right,

another to the left, one in
some second growth an
eighth of a mile further
on and the fourth troop
in plain sight, camped
near a little spring.

The Japs think they are
clever at ambush and the
troop was all strung out
at various tasks. The idea
was that the Big Swords
would see the troop,
think they had caught a

Boston Bean

small Jap outfit in the open and come charging in to wipe
them out and instead—get wiped out themselves. Major
Shiga and Major Yura were with the troop in the open.
Shiga wanted the glory of killing or capturing Captain
Cordie all for himself. Yura didn't care which of the Amer-
icans he got. He wanted them all.

"Here they come," Major Shiga said, softly, about four
o'clock in the afternoon. "See, they commence to filter
through the timber. Truly they must be fools to think that
we do not see them. Look, more come."

"It is time to start the first act," Major Yura answered,
rising.

"They know we see them." He jumped to his feet, raised
his arm and pointed, shouting commands. The Jap troop
went into defense formation.

They made no attempt to get to their horses. It was as if
they realized there would not be time to do it. Several of
the Big Swords rode boldly out in the open, halted, looked

the Jap troop over calmly, then looked back towards the timber. "They wait for the rest," Major Shiga announced. "Then they will charge as they always do."

"There are two of the Yankees coming out of the timber on the left. One of them is Captain Cordie. At last you charge to your death, Yankee dog."

"I had much rather that he be captured, Major Yura. Lieutenant Colonel Nagayo would give much to—"

MACHINE GUNS OPENED fire on the Japanese decoy troop, the two concealed left and right and combed the undergrowth for the fourth troop. A moment later the horses of the three troops came out of the blind canyon on the run. Something had stampeded them. They were more or less on a line with the horses of the decoy troop who now were plunging and rearing as several of them went down killed or wounded by machine gun bullets.

Why the stampeded horses did it, cannot be known but they swerved and ran in among the tied horses and just before they did it they ran through the Jap troop. Through and over them. Three hundred odd horses on the loose can cause a lot of trouble if they don't pay any attention to where they are going as fast as they can. The little Jap troopers were bowled over like tenpins, every which way. And the machine gun bullets singing the death song did not help any, either.

Major Yura got hit by a bullet squarely between the eyes and went down. Major Shiga was more lucky. He jumped to one side to avoid a horse, another horse upset him and a third kicked him in the head as he tried to get up. It was a glancing blow, not hard enough to break his skull but plenty hard enough to put him out.

The two troops left and right rose from where they had been lying in a little depression. That was all they could do unless they wanted to lie there as prone targets for machine gun bullets that had the proper angle to reach them. There was only one thing they could do and that was to get up and try to take the machine guns. Their officers snarled orders, they deployed into line of skirmish and started, one to the right and the other to the left. The machine gun fire was accurate and sustained and trooper after trooper fell before the charges got well started.

The Japs were caught in the open with carbines and revolvers. The sabers had been left attached to the saddles, Major Yura figuring the Big Swords could and would be wiped out by carbine fire and that the sabers would be useless encumbrances. Why he did not keep his squadron mounted and charge the Big Swords when they reached the clearing, one troop to each side, only Major Yura could explain. It may be that he had some good reason. If he made a mistake, he had paid for it with his life.

The decoy troop was out of commission as a fighting unit, the troopers left running to join the charge against the machine guns. The troop in the second growth came running out of it. It may not have been anything but a rearward movement, the Japanese claiming that they never retreat. But it certainly looked as if this time they had the rearward movement mixed up with a good old fashioned retreat.

Of course it is possible that they were charging out to reinforce their comrades and the line of Manchu swordsmen that appeared from the second growth had nothing to do with it. Many of the troopers were new recruits, some few veterans. The veterans for the most part, knew what the Manchu charging shout meant. The recruits had never heard it but something told them that it would sound much better from a distance. Whatever it was, the troop came out and right after them came seventy-five dismounted Big Swords. All Manchus and all swordsmen of the House of Chi. The Jap officers saw that the Big Swords would catch up to the troop so they turned the troopers to face the Manchus. There were, all told, eighty odd Jap troopers unwounded.

It was a messy fight, the little Japs standing right to it. But the Manchus had closed with them before many shots could be fired from the carbines. The machine guns that were on the troop ceased firing and joined the others concentrated on the two remaining troops.

No outfit of eighty men can whip seventy-five Manchu swordsmen if the Manchus are within sword reach and the Japanese cavalry found that fact out. Against the lightning fast upward and inward slash of the master swords the Jap had their carbine and revolvers. At that, when the Manchu line surged forward once more over the bodies of the troopers, fifty of the Manchus remained on the ground, dead or wounded so badly they could not get up. Which shows that the Japs are fighting men.

WHAT WAS LEFT of the two troops was faring badly, very badly. Ten Browning machine guns were full on them, four of the guns operated by the Bean, the Yid, Red Dolan and Carewe. The Bean and the Yid boasted that they could give a clean shave and a close haircut with their guns at five hundred yards and never miss a hair or cut the skin. Red topped that by insisting that when he was going good he could "shoot the claws off a titmouse wan mile away without hurtin' the little feller." Carewe, being English, never boasted of his skill or drew the long bow but as a matter of fact, he was as good a man with a machine gun as any of the three and maybe, a little better. Where machine gun operating was a topic of conversation, the four of them, all boasting to one side, were known to be aces.

The Japs were charging east and west against machine guns but other guns opened on them from the north and south. They were boxed in and the few officers left, knew it. The dismounted Big Swords were getting close, too close for the comfort of the gunners.

A bugle blew "cease firing, cease firing," and the machine guns immediately obeyed.

"Vot de hell now?" demanded the Yid, peevishly, rising from behind his gun. "Ve got dem vare dey live. Vat de hell is de—"

The Bean, whose gun was near the Yid's, answered, as he rose also. "I fully agree with you, my distinguished friend from Hester Street. But—

"Mr. Cohen, how about the Manchus and—yeah? I thought so! Look at Jimmie and George going in with fifteen men. There goes Red and his helpers. Come on, Yid!"

Jimmie Cordie and George Grigsby were charging, mounted, with twelve or fifteen Big Swords. Out from the machine guns came the soldiers of fortune and the Manchus who had been trained to operate one.

The Japs were being closed in on by a line of twenty-five swordsmen, dismounted, fifteen odd mounted and several units of two or three men, some armed with .45

Colt revolvers and some with the razor sharp Manchu swords.

The Japs were spread out a lot, about sixty or seventy of them. They saw foes coming from all sides. All officers had gone down and the non-coms now in command did not seem to know what to do. The troopers bunched as best they could to meet the dismounted Big Swords who were nearest. Again there was a messy fight for a minute or so and then the mounted Big Swords reached the Japs. Two minutes later, those of the Japs that could, broke and ran for the horse line of the decoy troop to which, although it was down on the ground, there were still some horses who could not break loose. What they did could not be called a rearward movement, in all deference to all Nippon.

A few of the troopers reached the horses, got them loose and rode away, most of them did not. A Japanese cavalry squadron had been practically wiped out.

"Let them go," Jimmie Cordie commanded, as the mounted Big Swords tightened up reins to pursue. "Most of them are only kids."

"They were old enough to account for a lot of Big Swords, Jimmie," Grigsby said, as he looked at what was left of the Manchus.

"That was then and this is now," Jimmie answered. "Then they were fighting men, now they are kids running for their lives."

"Oi," the Yid said, with a smirk. "Vat noble sentiments. I have it de same, gentlemen—und you also Mistaie Dolan. First ve fight dem und den ve kiss dem. Vonce in—"

"What? Gentlemen and me also? What ye need, ye

benighted Hester Street gibbon, is a good kiss right on the smacker by the fist ave me. For wan cent I'd—"

"Somevon give it Red a cent. I ain't got no change."

"It might get him into trouble," Jimmie said, with a grin. "I'm glad you and I feel alike, Abie. Let's pick up our wounded and get out of here. There may be some more Jap squadrons waiting to play with us. I think two or three Big Swords went down near the horse line."

6

NARROW ESCAPE

MAJOR SHIGA CAME slowly out of the darkness. His head was aching badly and he could hardly open his eyes. The last thing he remembered was a horse knocking him down. He got his eyes open and sat up. Within fifty feet of him, a group of riders sat on their saddles. Men were searching the welter of dead and dying men and horses. Shiga looked around, his eyes almost popping out of his head. The squadron had been destroyed and—there sat Captain Cordie on a horse! Captain Cordie and the other Yankees! Now was his chance. He would rise, draw his revolver and kill Captain Cordie! He would die the next instant himself but what of that? Forgotten was Colonel Takara, the American killer and all else. He, Major Shiga, would kill Captain Cordie.

He waited a moment or so until strength came back to him and then rose to his feet. No one paid any attention to him. There were a good many Japs staggering around, those who had suffered broken arms when the horses ran over them and those who had only been slightly wounded by the machine gun fire. They made no attempt to give battle and so, had been let alone.

His right hand stole to his service revolver and closed

on the butt. Captain Cordie presented a good target and Major Shiga knew that he, Shiga, a champion pistol shot, would not miss at fifty feet. He drew the gun and leveled it. Right there is where he made a mistake that cost him the use of his right hand for as long as he lived. If he had drawn and fired from the hip he might have got Jimmie Cordie. But he was used to taking plenty of time and aiming at a target.

The Boston Bean, by chance or by direction of the Red Gods of War, had turned a little in the saddle and saw the gun rising to the level the Jap wanted it. The Bean's action was automatic. He drew, fired as the muzzle of his .45 Colt cleared the holster, shooting at the hand that held the gun. He knew that if he fired at the Jap's body, the bullet might not kill instantly and a twitch of the finger would detonate the gun. Not that the Bean took out time to figure all that. It was included in the sub-conscious reaction.

The gun leaped from the hand of Major Shiga who stood there, looking down on his torn and mangled right hand, a dazed expression on his countenance.

As the Bean shot, or rather, a split second after he did, five other Colt revolvers appeared as if put in the hands of the men holding them by magic. Jimmie Cordie, the Yid, Red, George Grigsby and Carewe all drew, as automatically as the Bean had done, before they saw what the Bean had shot at so successfully.

"Over there," the Bean said, in a bored tone of voice. "One of those kids Jimmie was talking about. He was just going to kiss you, Jeems, with a bullet when I happened to see him."

"Yeah? The intire Cordie family thanks you, Codfisher. I'll go over and ask him what the heck he meant by it."

"Look at the little pink toe hellion standin' there proud and haughty. Wait, Jimmie, I'll teach the little bamalan to—"

"You will? When did you get an invite to the party? He was going to take a pot shot at me, wasn't he?"

As they started for Major Shiga, Jimmie went on. "He don't look proud and haughty to me. He looks a darn sight more sick and dizzy. That was rotten shooting, Bean. Couldn't you knock the gun out of his hand without taking part of the hand with it?"

The utterly reckless, devil may care soldiers of fortune all laughed at that, the Bean saying meekly, "I'll try and do better the next time, Captain dear."

THEY RODE UP to Shiga and Jimmie demanded, sternly, "What the heck is the giddy idea of taking a shot at me? Don't you know that the fight is over—and you a major?" He didn't know whether the Jap could speak or understand English or not. If he couldn't, Jimmie would have tried Pushtu, the universal language of the border.

"I tried to kill you, Captain Cordie, because you have—you have—my hand bleeds my life away. I—of the Shiga—will always try to kill you for the—honor of Nippon and—"

"Wait until I fix your hand up," Jimmie answered with a grin, as he dismounted. "You couldn't try to kill a sick canary bird right now."

"You—will treat my hand? You, the Yankee—"

"Why not? I like to have the gents who try for me, physically in good condition. Get off, Yid, and break open your

"You Yankee dog! You will not escape this time!"

first aid kit. Sit down, Major, and take it easy. You're all right. Relax yourself."

"Wait. This I tell you, Captain Cordie. No matter whether you treat my wound or not—I will capture or kill you and the mongrels with you at—"

"You mean if you can—and don't call names, Major. We are not in position to resent it. Hold your hand out."

"I—I—if I did not wish to live and some day—"

"Yeah, I know. Hold out your hand. Remember, 'he who fights and runs away, will live to fight another day.' You didn't run away, but you are going to ride away. Think of 'another day,' old timer."

It was a half an hour later when Jimmie said, "Well, I guess that does it."

Twice Major Shiga had to be fed brandy, that the Yid could always produce in some miraculous fashion, before Jimmie could go on. Jimmie was no doctor, any more than any of the soldiers of fortune were doctors, but they were all good first aid men and all of them had years of experience with wounds. So Major Shiga's hand was saved for him, although he never used it again.

"And now," Jimmie went on, "you can mount and ride away or stick right here with your wounded. I have a feeling that it won't be long before there will be some of your boy friends up here to take a look see. We would dearly love to stay and welcome them but—you know, Major, duty calls and love must obey."

"You joke, Captain Cordie? Know that soon you will be—"

"Who the hell are ye to be threatenin' the betters ave ye, ye little bamalam midget?" interrupted Red. "Ye sit there as if ye amounted to more than a half pint ave nawthin. Wan good man can lick wan hundred ave ye wid wan hand tied behind—"

"Put a jaw tackle on, Red. They don't think as we do—about lots of things.

"Are you going to ride, Major?"

"No, I remain here. I will remember what you said, Red, and some day, call your attention to it."

"Aw—says ye, that all. Run along home, bamalam, and the next time keep out ave the way ave real men."

"Don't answer him, Red. Major, I would suggest that you realize the position you are in and—curb your tongue. Who commanded the squadron? You haven't the cavalry insignia. Who was your ranking officer?"

"Major Yura. He lies there—dead."

"That's too bad. I was going to ask you to pass the word to him if he escaped, that it is bad policy to detail rank and file troopers to scout a Big Swords column. Especially when there are Manchu hillmen with the column. And to put horses in a blind canyon and arrange a decoy right in front of the entrance is also not so good. Something might scare the horses. You may pass it along to cavalry leaders."

"You—you have the effrontery to offer advice to—"

"Well, some one has got to do it. From all I've seen, you Japanese need advice badly. Are you set?"

"Am I what?"

"Pardon me, Major. I mean, are you now in condition to await your friends?"

"Yes."

"Then we will ride. Good-by, Major. Better luck next time, perhaps."

Major Shiga looked at the soldiers of fortune who stood looking at him out of mocking, intolerant eyes. Finally he snarled, "Good-by."

As Jimmie Cordie mounted, he called over, "Oh, by the way, Major, give my regards to Lieutenant-General Nagayo, if you run across him. Tell him I congratulate him on his promotion."

"And tell the little scut that if I lay the two hands ave me on him I'll twist the scrawny neck ave him all the way off," Red added, as the Big Swords officers rode away.

7

FEIGNED CAPTURE

"WHY SHOULD I do that?" asked old Mangali Boga, Khan of the Badakshan. "You are up to some trick—as ever." Jimmie Cordie, who was sitting crosslegged on a rug in the Khan's tent, grinned cheerfully.

He and the old Khan were, if not friends, at least old acquaintances. At one time, the Badakshan Tartars had called upon the Uryankhes Tartars for help in tribal warfare. Jimmie Cordie at the time was with the Uryankhes. Together the Uryankhes and the Badakshan mopped up on the foe. Later, the Badakshan, intoxicated by success, tried out the Uryankhes, their former allies. They found out that fighting with the Uryankhes as allies was quite different from fighting against the Uryankhes.

The Uryankhes chased the Badakshan back into the hills until tired of the sport. So, Mangali Boga and Jimmie Cordie knew each other full well. They were talking in Pushtu.

"Certainly I am up to a trick," Jimmie answered, calmly. "But it is not a trick against you, mighty Khan of the peerless Badakshan."

"How do I know that?" asked the suspicious, wary old

fighter. "You have nothing to swear by, being one of the English."

Mangali Boga had never heard of America or Americans but he had seen Englishmen and classed Jimmie as one.

"I don't have to do any swearing of oaths. It is simple, what I ask of you. You will take us into San-sing or Shuntien as prisoners, roped together. You will tell the men of Nippon that you captured us en route. They will ask you for us. You will refuse to give us up saying that we killed many of the Badakshan before being captured. You will keep us under guard in the heart of your encampment. We will come and go, under cover of the darkness until—"

"I will do all that? The trick, then, is against the men of Nippon. What is to prevent me taking you to them? It may be that they would pay well for Big Swords officers."

"Not a doubt in the world. They would pay you much gold. The only trouble is that Sahet Khan of the Uryankhes might not like to have his blood brother sold to the men of Nippon. I am afraid he might lose his temper, as he has done before. Of course, if you don't mind a blood feud with the Uryankhes and incidentally with the Big Swords, you can get much gold for us, as I say."

"Ho! I am not afraid of the Uryankhes or of the Big Swords either," lied Mangali Boga lustily. He was afraid of the Uryankhes and he did not want any trouble with the Manchu swordsmen of Chang-lung Liang, either.

"I know that," Jimmie also lied. "I said they might not like it."

"I would not do such a thing and you know it, Captain

Cordie. I am of the blood of the Emperor of All Men, Genghis Khan."

"I also know that. It shows plainly in your face and in your bearing. All you have to do is to pay no attention to our coming and going and at last you find—we have escaped. What could be simpler and more easy to do for a friend."

"And after the trick on the little men of Nippon has been played, what then will they say to me who comes to them as an ally?"

"You don't know about any trick. All you know is that some prisoners you held have escaped. Are you afraid of the little men of Nippon?"

"Yes," answered Mangali Boga, frankly, "I am, while there are so many of them."

"How many men have you?"

"Ten thousand. The little men of Nippon told me to bring all I could. I am to receive so much a day for them."

"And most of them will be slain, probably all of them. Will the little men of Nippon keep on paying for them, so much a day?"

"You know better. I am also afraid of you and your tricks. I will not do what you ask."

"Would you do it if Chang-lung Liang of the House of Chi asked you to do it?"

"No."

"Would you do it if in addition to asking you he would say to you as follows, 'You, Mangali Boga, may choose the ten strongest men of your tribe and with them enter the treasure house of the House of Chi. There you and they may pick out what you desire and with it, walk unmolested away.' I know there are things there, Mangali Boga, that were once with your great ancestor Genghis Khan in Samarkand."

"How do you know?"

I HAVE BEEN in the treasure house and seen them. The tree made of jade, the fruit of precious stones, the birds of—"

"Let him tell me that. His word is good, that I know. With ten men I can carry away twenty times what the little men of Nippon offer me. Let him, Chang-lung Liang, tell me that and I will do whatever you say."

"Do you also know Ch'ienlung, his nephew, who some day will become the Head of the House of Chi?"

"Yes, I know him. Many times have I traded with the House of Chi before the little men of Nippon came."

"If he delivered the message to you and swore on the honor of the House of Chi that it was true word of Chang-lung Liang, would you accept it as such?"

"Yes, without question."

"He is here with me. I will call him and have him deliver the message. In turn you must swear on the Yassa of Genghis Khan that you will do as I order until I release you from further obedience." The "Yassa" is the code of laws or conduct written by Genghis Khan.

"I will swear it. Go and get Ch'ienlung."

"Wait until we get it clear. You are to take us in as prisoners—refuse to give us up. Allow us to come and go as we see fit, and when we escape, if we do, you know nothing save some prisoners escaped. Nothing the little men of Nippon say or offer makes any impression on you. We have killed Badakshan tribesmen in the hills and so, die in the hills. If the little men ask you why you did not slay us at once, say that you have sent for the relations of the dead men so that they may be present while we are being tortured."

"That is clear. What if the little men of Nippon attack me?"

"They won't, openly. They know that if they did all tribes would be afraid to join them. They may try to cut us out but I doubt it."

"That is true. I will go as far as you have said, but no further. Then, after you have escaped or been slain through no fault of mine, I can enter the House of Chi treasure house with ten men and carry away all we wish."

"Yes."

"Get Ch'ienlung, Captain Cordie. You have made a trade."

LIEUTENANT-GENERAL NAGAYO OF the Japanese High Command had come up to Sansing from Tsitsihar. He heard of what the Big Swords had done to the cavalry squadron and it had not at all improved his temper, which generally was bad.

He ordered that Major Shiga report to him, as soon as released from the hospital, and was talking to Colonel Takara when Major Shiga came in. The Major's hand was bandaged and carried in a sling. He saluted with his left hand and stood at attention.

"Tell me just what happened when the cavalry squadron commanded by Major Yura, met the Big Swords column," Nagayo rasped.

Major Shiga told him, finishing with "and when I returned to the land of the living, the squadron had been destroyed."

"I know that the squadron was destroyed. Wounded troopers have said that after you got on your feet, you—tell me in detail just what you did?"

"I saw Captain Cordie of the Big Swords and the other Yankee dogs, within a few feet of me, sitting on their horses," Shiga went on, finishing with "Captain Cordie called to me, 'Give my regard to Lieutenant-General Nagayo if you run across him. Tell him I congratulate him on his promotion,' and then—"

"Captain Cordie flirts always with death. Some day it will amount to more than a flirtation. Now he has taken it upon himself to advise us. He himself rides to a fall and soon. There is no blame attached to you, Major Shiga. You made a gallant effort to kill him and—if you had been just a little bit faster," he added, sneeringly, "you might have succeeded in doing so."

Major Shiga did not like Nagayo and never had, principally on account of Nagayo's overbearing ways. The Nagayo clan in Nippon was not nearly as important as the Shiga and Major Shiga resented the tone of Nagayo's voice.

"There was one other thing said, General," he went on, smoothly. "As you have asked me for details, I will repeat it. The one called 'Red' also called out, 'and tell the little scut that if I lay the two hands ave me on him I'll twist the scrawny neck all the way off.' Those are the exact words, General."

Lieutenant-General Nagayo, figuratively, hit the ceiling. He cursed all Americans, America, all soldiers of fortune in general and Jimmie Cordie and Red Dolan in particular. After he cooled down a little he said, "I was going back to Tokyo for a visit but now, by the honor of the Nagayo clan

I will stay and hunt them down. I will take one division or six if necessary and exterminate the Big Swords once for all and as I do, I will—"

A staff captain entered and saluted. "What is it?" Nagayo demanded, barely returning the salute.

"The Khan of the Badakshan goes into camp near the river, General, and with—"

"Am I to be interrupted because a hillman goes into camp? You have a strange idea of the fitness of things."

"I was about to report, General, that the Khan of the Badakshan has with him, as prisoners, several Big Swords officers."

"What! Who are they, do you know?"

"They are the Yankees who fight for the Big Swords. Captain Cordie, the Fighting Yid, the—"

"Mangali Boga has them? You are sure, Captain Mito?"

"Yes, General, I have but just come from there. The Khan of the Badakshan has them, six of them. The ones who defended—"

"I know what they defended. Come with me, Colonel Takara—and you also Major Shiga. Mangali Boga will give or sell them to us and then we will see how much advice Captain Cordie has to offer when a rope is around his neck and—" Nagayo continued, almost to the Badakshan camp, telling what was going to happen once he had "the cursed Yankee mongrels."

On the way, Colonel Takara had a chance to say to Major Shiga, "It looks as if we must be content with the glory that is well within our grasp, Major."

"Yes, Colonel. I wish it were otherwise but—the pleasure of seeing Captain Cordie dancing on thin air will assuage

my disappointment a good deal. It must be that they ran
into the Badakshan after destroying the squadron."

8

JIMMIE AND NAGAYO MEET AGAIN

JIMMIE CORDIE, THE Yid, the Bean, Red Dolan, Grigsby and Carewe sat on the ground near the center of the Badakshan camp. Their belts were empty of cartridges, their holsters empty of guns and their hands were tied behind their backs. They were sitting in a line, their backs to the side of a tent.

"What the hell now?" Red growled. "How long do we have to sit here? The scut that tied these ropes pulled them too tight. Jimmie, can't we smoke?"

"What? The bad old hillmen took everything we had off us. What do you want to do, crab the works? Be a regular prisoner, you big ape."

"Come over here und sit it by Poppa, little von," the Yid said. "Und Poppa vill sing it a nice song und put de baby to sleep."

"Oh, ye will? I dare ye to come widin reach ave the foot ave me, ye Hester Street gibbon. 'Tis Poppa who will go to sleep, ye beneath notice Yid ave the world."

"That's the boy, Red," the Bean encouraged, sleepily. "Tell him just who he is. I'm wid ye—me good man."

"And who the hell gave you a invite to—"

"Here comes—holy cats! It's our old friend Nagayo in

62

person. Look at the grin on his face. The cat that swallowed the canary has nothing on our dear Lieutenant-General. Hivings help the poor woiking goil if old Mangali Boga don't play ball. Begin sounding off, Red, about the Badakshan, our getting captured and things in general."

"I will, Jimmie. And what the hell good was it for us to mop up on a lot of the pink toed bamalams and then—"

"Not so strong about the Japs," Jimmie warned. "They might get so mad that they'll take us whether or no."

"It as ye say, Jimmie," shouted Red. " 'Tis worse than bamalams they are. What are they are all by a lot of little yellow monkeys on sticks? They can't invent nawthin— they only copy the—"

"Well, you redheaded ape. Some day I'll hang one on you for that."

Jimmie was talking in a low tone of voice and Red was shouting, being plainly heard by Nagayo and the other two Intelligence officers, plus several line officers who had joined the party on hearing that Big Swords officers had been captured.

"That's right, Jimmie," the Yid also shouted. "By golly gumpers, vot a true statement. Dey licked it de Russians ven de Russians didn't have it no powder und only pewter bayonets und von gun to five men. Who else did dey ever lick? De Chinks stopped it dem at Shanghai und—oi, vot have de Big Swords did to dem time und again."

"Yeah? Backing Mr. Dolan right up, aren't you, Mr. Cohen? I hope the Japs take the both of you out and—"

"Vell, vell," the Yid said, cheerfully, as Nagayo and the other Jap officers halted in front of the seated line of prisoners, "look who is here. Oi, Red, look vot de cat brought in."

All of the Japs could understand English and their little beady eyes flamed hot with wrath as more than one hand went to pistol butt.

"I don't have to look at it," snarled Red, "I can smell it. What kind of monkeys are they, Abie?"

"No, gentlemen," Nagayo said, with a laugh, "take your hands away. It is only Red Dolan and the Fighting Yid talking. Does a fast train stop to lesson a little mongrel yapping beside the tracks? We meet—"

"Who the hell do ye think ye are, ye pint sized black and white kitty?" Red interrupted. "Ye stand there grinnin' like ye amounted to something—all of ye. Wan good man could chase ye back up trees, ye—"

"That's plenty, Red. That goes for you also, Yid. I'll take it over. You were saying, General?"

Jimmie Cordie and Lieutenant General Nagayo had met several times before, when the lieutenant general was a colonel.

"I started to say, Captain Cordie, that you and I meet again. Do you think you will again escape me?"

"Well, I have before and—what is written, is written. Were you made a Lieutenant-General for your—er—recent campaign against the Big Swords?"

"I—I—you Yankee dog! You will not escape this time. Soon you will feel a rope tighten around your neck and—"

"I never have yet. Does it hurt very much?"

"Speakin' ave necks," Red put in, "did ye get the message I sent ye by the little bamalam midget standin' there as if he was a man? Listen, get the wildman to order me untied and ye can have the sword and revolver ave ye. Ye will see how it feels to have a pair ave hands around the chicken neck ave ye, me bucko giniril."

"Captain Dolan seems peeved, Captain Cordie. It may be that being finally taken by an insignificant hill tribe has shown him how truly—"

MANGALI BOGA CAME up. "What do you men of Nippon do here with my prisoners?" he demanded suspiciously. "Why did you not come first to me?"

"We were told that you were away, mighty Khan," answered Nagayo in Pushtu. "And so, not thinking that you would object we went to see the famous Big Swords that you, the clever one, have been able to capture where others failed."

"All of you men of Nippon speak with a smooth tongue," answered Mangali Boga scornfully. "You have seen them— now go. I will attend to them when the proper time comes."

"We know that, ruler of the hills. Yet, it may be that—I crave the honor of an audience with you, oh Khan of the Badakshan."

"Come with me, then."

"You gentlemen return to headquarters. The Khan of the Badakshans honors me with an audience."

As Nagayo left with Mangali Boga the Bean asked Major Shiga, "How's your hand, Major?"

"My hand is getting well but I will never be able to use it again, thanks to you. You are he who is called the 'Boston Bean,' are you not?"

"Sure he is," answered the Yid, with a smirk. "Dot's him. De Bean or de Codfisher or—"

"What are ye talkin' to the little bamalam for?" Red

asked, contemptuously. "Go on away from us, ye pink toed midget before I get up and blow ye away wid wan breath."

"Can you beat that, George?" Jimmie Cordie asked, wearily.

"I reckon it doesn't make much difference, Jimmie. We are gone coons, anyway. Mangali Boga intends to skin us alive up in the hills, from what I overheard. It seems we killed too many tribesmen."

"We will spare you that fate," Major Shiga said, with an evil smile on his lips. "I do not know what is meant by 'gone coons,' but you, who once were Big Swords officers, are surely—gone coons, if it means you are about to die a cur's death."

"Don't count the chickens before they're hatched, ye—I'm shut, Jimmie darlin'."

"I won't," Major Shiga returned, "although I am quite sure it is—what is the expression? Oh, yes, it is in the bag. I learned that in the land that you will never see again—and which we will soon see over our gun sights."

"Send some gentlemen over that can draw much faster than you can, Major," the Bean drawled, "otherwise—I am afraid—there will be very little sight-seeing."

"You—you—I will see to it that you are—let us go, gentlemen."

"Goodbye," called the Yid after them. "Come und see us again sometime. De latch string alvays hangs it on de outside."

The Japanese officers marched haughtily away without answering. Jimmie grinned, "Well—that's that. Now, if old Mangali Boga hangs tough, to-night we'll start looking for Mr. Chapman."

MANGALI BOGA DID "hang tough," much to Nagayo's disgust. Nothing that Nagayo could offer had any effect on the old Khan. No, he would not turn over the prisoners to the Japanese. No, he would not name a price for them. No, he would not publicly execute them. They had slain Badakshan tribesmen and he had sent for the relations of the slain men to come and witness what was done to the slayers.

It was an old Badakshan custom. He would take the Big Swords to the hills, to the place they had slain the tribesmen and there make them wish a wolf had stolen them from the cradle, or words to that effect. And if the Japs bothered him he would start for the hills now and not come back. He was a friend of General Oakia and had promised that he would fight against bandits and what-not for the Japs but by so and so, he would not wait until General Oakia came from Nippon if he could not hold a few prisoners without being asked for them.

All in all, Nagayo left the old Khan feeling as if he, Nagayo, could more than cheerfully wipe out all hillmen and the Badakshan tribe of hillmen first of all. He had one ray of hope and that was that General Oakia could get Mangali Boga to unbelt where he, Nagayo, could not. He did not dare force an open break with the old Khan and he knew that if the Japs tried anything else but bribery or persuasion, Mangali Boga would make the break himself. One thing he could do and that was to see to it that no Big Swords rescue column reached the prisoners.

9

INFORMATION AT A PRICE

THAT NIGHT, THE prisoners were fed, after being untied, and herded into the tent. The Badakshan tribesmen, in general, did not know what it was all about. They had seen the Big Swords ride calmly into the hill camp and a good many of them recognized Jimmie Cordie. They had seen their Khan greet him and later had seen the Manchus ride away leaving the white men. The next morning they saw the white men bound and placed on horses.

Word had been passed that they were prisoners of Mangali Boga, that they had slain Badakshan tribesmen and also that no tribesman knew anything else if questioned by the little men of Nippon. That was sufficient to close all mouths, all the tribesmen knowing what would happen to them if they disobeyed an order of old Mangali Boga.

"Well," Red announced, "here we are. Now what, Jimmie? Are we goin' to hunt for the scut?"

"We have got to do that little thing, Mr. Dolan. I'm frank to say that it does not look quite so good right here as it did up in the Big Swords camp. This darn place is full of Japs and—"

"What did you think it would be, Jeems, me good man?" asked the Bean, lazily, "full of platinum blondes?"

"Oi, dot vos a hot von, Codfisher. Sure he did. Full mit—"

"You know, George, I think it a good idea to send the Yid and the Bean out first. If they don't last more than ten minutes we'll know that something is wrong and make new plans."

" 'Tis a good idea, Jimmie darlin'," Red agreed, promptly. "What the hell are they but a couple ave beneath notice ring tailed monkeys?"

"Why throw us to the lions, Jeems? Try them out with Mr. Dolan. If the Japs don't catch him, they can't catch anything."

"Let's quit fooling around for a change and get down to cases," Grigsby said. "The first act went over, Jimmie. But from what I saw on the way in—not so good. Any one of us out hunting for Chapman in this man's town has about as much chance as a lame dog in a running match."

"I've come to that conclusion myself, George. I saw heap plenty officers here that I know have fussed around with us at close quarters two or three times."

"Well, how did ye think ye was goin' to do?" demanded Red, impatiently.

"I thought that there would be more civilians here, Red, and more tribesmen who have thrown in with Misto Jap. The Badakshan seem to be the only ones around at the moment, as far as I can see. George, you and I, or Carewe and I might chief ourselves up as Badakshan tribesmen and—"

"What? How about me, ye black muzzled shrimp? Am I to be left suckin' the thumb ave me while ye—"

"There it starts. Did we ever in our lives have to pick out who is—"

Mangali Boga came into the tent, very well pleased with himself about the way he had handled Lieutenant General Nagayo.

"I have kept my word, Captain Cordie." The little man of Nippon walked away, muttering to himself. "What now?"

"Two of us must leave the camp to-night and search for that for which we came, mighty one. We are deciding which two shall go. And also how to disguise ourselves so that we are not recognized."

"I have nothing to do with that. I will send one to you who will see to it that you clear my lines without hindrance. How you go—and when you return is not my concern. Except—if two go and do not return, what then?"

"Why—then two more will go. If they do not return, two more. If any of us are captured or slain by the little men of Nippon, you are not, as you said, concerned, Khan of the Badakshan. We all know the trick we try to play and will keep on as long as there is one of us alive. If we are all wiped out, you are released and may go to the treasure house of Chi as soon as you see fit. Until that time comes—you will continue as you are doing until you are told by any one of us that the end has come for your help. Is that plain?"

"Yes," answered the old Khan, grimly, very plain." He turned and stalked out of the tent.

AFTER HE HAD gone, the Yid said, "I tell you vot, Jimmie.

Make it up de Irisher as a potato und ve will throw him over de—"

"For Pete's sake! Listen, you Yid chimpanzee. Disguise yourself as a clam and fool all of us. You also, Codfisher? I want to try and figure things out and I'll be darned if I can if you two are going to dribble off at the mouth all the time."

"Was I saying anything?" the Bean asked, deeply grieved.

"No, but you looked as if you might start any minute. George, I think the best thing we can do is to sleep on it. There is no use going off half-cocked. My brain seems to be made of mush at the moment."

"I say, that's a good idea, what, what, what? In the daylight many things look different, old dears, than they do at night. We may see some way to fool the jolly little blighters tomorrow that we do not see to-night."

"That's right, Carewe," Grigsby agreed. "If we can only think up some way to muzzle the Yid and the Bean so as to get some sleep."

"Why leave the redheaded mick out?" inquired the Bean. "He is the one that generally starts the argument."

"There you go starting it. Let's cut it out and get some sleep. No more wah wah, gents. Commanding officer speaking."

They did get a little sleep but not very much. The blankets tossed in by the guards posted over them by Mangali Bogo were, to put it mildly, not quite free from insect life.

The next morning, after they were fed, their hands were again tied behind their backs.

"What now?" Red snarled.

"Sit beside the tent," Jimmie answered, "we have some more visitors."

"Why can't we smoke?"

"Go ahead if you have any tobacco and can get your hands loose," Jimmie said, with a grin, as he sat down.

"Yeah? Go ahead, banty. 'Tis daylight and everything. Go ahead and see some way to fool the bamalams. I don't want to sit here all day wid the hands ave me tied behind me back."

At that, they all laughed and Jimmie said, "Give him a few minutes, Red. In the meantime look around yourself."

"Me? What the hell do I know about it? Here we are. Is the brain ave ye still mush, Jimmie Cordie?"

"The fact that he asks you to look around, me good man, shows conclusively that it is," the Bean said.

"Is what, ye long legged beanpole from Bosting?"

"Still mush."

"What? Ye sit there and say that the brain ave Jimmie Cordie is mush, ye misbegotten cross between a telegraph pole and a jacksnipe? Who the hell are ye to—"

"Shut up, Red. Look at those Chinese peddlers over by Mangali Boga's tent. Maybeso there is a T'aip'ing among 'em. If there is we will darn soon find out where Chapman is without hunting around for him."

Jimmie Cordie got up and walked over to where the guards were sitting around a campfire.

"Is it permitted that the Chinese merchants come over and show us what they have to sell?"

A sub Khan answered, "Why not? Have you money to buy, you who led the Uryankhes with Sahet against us."

"Only to stop the Badakshan from doing what they

said they would not. Go and tell the Chinese to come over here."

"Why should I? I take orders from Mangali Boga, not from you, Englishman."

"Take this order from me, mighty swordsman. And also—take this." Jimmie Cordie took from his finger a jade ring set with an emerald, given him by a Manchu noble. "Wear it and when, in the future, you need a friend, show it to me, or to any Big Swords."

"That is different," the sub Khan grunted, rising, and held out his hand for the ring. "I will bring them to you."

"One at a time," Jimmie ordered.

The first Chinese peddler was brought up. Jimmie Cordie's Chinese was more than sketchy but he did the best he could, "You know me, little brother?"

"No."

"I am the black eyed, smiling one, honorable elder brother of the all powerful Head, Yen Yuan. Now do you know me?"

"No. I know nothing of all powerful heads or of you."

"Take him back and bring me another," Jimmie said in Pushtu to the sub Khan. Another Chinese was brought and then another and another. None of them responded.

The fifth Chinese was a member of the most powerful and dreaded secret society in the Orient, the T'aip'ing. All over the world, wherever there are Chinese, there are T'aip'ing members. The society numbers over four million members and to all of them, the orders of the "Head" are obeyed to the letter. No Chinese, in their sane senses, would any more think of disobeying a T'aip'ing order or a gently voiced request, than they would of stepping with bare feet on a cobra.

The fifth Chinese answered, "Give orders, resplendent one, I have never before been dazzled by your splendor, but I have been told of the order."

"How many of the society are within call?"

"That I do not know, Lord of the World. I know of twenty odd here and in Ksinking, Fang Wu, a war captain is in Shuntien."

"I know him. My orders are these. Go to Fang Lu. Tell him that the black eyed smiling one is here. Tell him I order a search made for a white man named Chapman who is being held in hiding by the little men of Nippon somewhere close to Shuntien. The little men are not to know that the search is being made. Fang Lu is to report to me, here."

"As you order, honorable elder brother."

"You have my permission to depart."

"DID YE FIND wan?" Red asked as Jimmie came back and sat down.

"I did, Mr. Dolan. Stick around a little while. We will know where Chapman is held before dark."

"Then what?"

"Why then, George and I will go and see him."

"George and you? What the hell is the matter wid me goin' wid ye?"

"It is my hunt, Red," Grigsby answered, quietly. "There are two or three questions I want to ask him regarding his treatment of a kinswoman of mine."

"In other words, Mr. Dolan," the Bean explained, "there

is a Grigsby-Chapman feud on. The Dolans, not bein' feudists, are not invited."

"Listen to me. The Dolans was feudists, whatever that
is, in Ireland long before there was beaneaters in Bosting
and—"

"Sit over next to him and tell him all about it," Jimmie
interrupted. "We'll go out as Chinks, George, with the
T'aip'ing."

"What are you going to do with the rotter?" asked
Carewe.

"I am going to kill him," Grigsby answered.

10

SURPRISE ATTACK

T'ANG LI, THE shopkeeper, was awakened by insistent knocking at the rear door of his shop. It was about three o'clock in the morning and a heavy rain beat against the windows. T'ang Li did not intend to open his shop, which dealt in leather goods, at any such time in the night so he raised a window a little and called, "Who is there?"

"It is I, Kwang Liu. I have something with me that is very valuable that was bought from a Manchu noble. Let me in and I will sell it to you very cheap."

"You mean stolen. I know you, Kwang Liu. What is it?"

"A saddle and bridle made of the finest leather embossed with jade and gold and silver. Quick, T'ang Li. It may get wet in spite of the covering."

T'ang Li fell for it. He knew what a Manchu saddle was worth and what it would bring from any Chinese war lord or general who happened to be in funds. He knew that Kwang Liu was a bandit and he had dealt with him before but what he didn't know was that Kwang Liu, in addition to all this, was a T'aip'ing.

It had not been very difficult for the T'aip'ing to find out that a white man was living above the shop of T'ang Li. That he had arrived in a wagon and was carried into the shop, either drunk, very sick or drugged. In some way word went around among the Chinese that "the mighty society desired to find a foreign devil in hiding somewhere close." Word that no Japanese could hear no matter how close they were or thought they were to Chinese friends and servants.

It was a matter concerning the T'aip'ing and so, save among themselves and then only in a vague, round about way, lips were sealed. A Chinese who had come with the wagon train mentioned something, an old woman, huddled against a wall for shelter had seen something and finally Fang Lu, a war captain of the T'aip'ing had reported to Jimmie Cordie, "The one you seek is in a room above the shop of a Chinese leather merchant named T'ang Li, honorable elder brother of the all powerful Head."

That night, Jimmie and Grigsby, disguised as Chinese peddlers, in the center of several of the T'aip'ing swords-men also posing as peddlers had left the Badakshan camp. The Japanese met on the way paid no attention to a few Chinese evidently on their way home after a hard day and evening's work trying to sell grimcracks to tribesmen.

"I will let you in. Is there anyone with you?"

"No. Hurry, T'ang Li."

The Chinese spy for the Japs opened the rear door, "Come in. I will look at the saddle in the daylight and—" Merciless hands closed around his throat, shutting off his wind before he could cry out. He was lowered to the floor and a dagger point pressed against his back. A snarled command told him not to move unless he wished to die. T'ang Li wished to live and he became like a frozen man.

Three more T'aip'ing came into the room with Jimmie Cordie and Grigsby.

"Up the stairs to the room on the left," Fang Lu directed.

The American was awake, sitting propped up with the pillows, in bed. There was a small kerosene lamp on a table near the bed which threw a little light. Chapman's face, in the light, looked gray. His eyes were dilated and his nostrils flared out. A moment before the door was opened, he had taken a "shot" of cocaine. Whatever else he was, he was no coward. There was no fear in his eyes as he glared at what to him were two Chinese.

"Get the hell out of here, you punks," he commanded. "What are you doing here?"

"Why," Jimmie Cordie answered, "a friend told us you were here and so, being Yanks, we came to call upon you."

Chapman, while Jimmie was speaking, stared at them as if not sure they were not visions conjured up by the snow in him.

"Get up out of that bed," Grigsby ordered, curtly.

Chapman knew then that the men confronting him were real. "Oh, yeah? That little louse better be careful who—"

HE MEANT TAKARA, but Grigsby thought he meant Betty Ann. Jimmie Cordie was going to try and lead Chapman on, to get the inside of what was going to happen by posing as killers looking for a job and so on. But Grigsby spoiled any chance Jimmie might have had.

"I am Elizabeth Ann Shelby's kinsman," Grigsby drawled. "Get on your feet. And after you do, reach for your gun!"

"What? Well—for the love of Mike! Kentucky stuff way

over here in China. Listen, you. To hell with Elizabeth Ann Shelby and to hell with you and to hell with your buddy here. What do you know about that? I haven't got a rod, punk. If I had, you'd be cold meat by now."

"Let him take yours, Jimmie."

"I will not. This thing that looks like a man is some copperhead snake. No use arguing with him or anything else. The drug has got him. Kill him—or I will, in the name of all the mothers and fathers whose—"

"Go ahead," jeered Chapman. "See if I care. Come on, get it over with. Turn the heat on, Kaintuck. I ain't got a rod or nothin'."

"Get back against the wall, Jimmie," Grigsby said, quietly, "I will use my bare hands to send him to the hell he belongs in."

Jimmie Cordie looked at Grigsby, "I will execute him, George. That is what it will be, an—" he laughed. "Hop right to it, Mr. Kinsman." As he said it, he backed to the wall.

"Now, you lowdown," Grigsby ordered, "get up and learn what it means to degrade a Shelby woman."

"How about it?" demanded Chapman of Jimmie. "Do I get an even break? I'll take this big house like Grant took Richmond. How about you—after?"

"Well—if you take George Grigsby, Mr. Chapman, I will walk out of this room after tucking you back in bed."

Jimmie Cordie knew that Grigsby was just about as strong and as fast as a grizzly bear.

"Fair enough. Here I come, big feller." Chapman had once been very fast on his feet and with his hands, packing a knockout in either one of them and the snow made him think he still did.

T'ANG LI HAD a small Chinese servant, a boy about eleven, who slept under a bench in the kitchen. The candle that T'ang Li had lighted and carried to the door, had dropped and gone out as hands closed on his throat. The T'aip'ing had relighted it and put it on the stove which was cold. There was very little light but T'ang Li did not need light to know that the dagger point was still at his back.

Three of the T'aip'ing, swords in hand, sat down on the bench without thinking to look under it. Nothing any bigger than the half-pint sized boy could have got under it, anyway.

He had been awakened by the commotion but instead of getting out from under the bench and running, he had hugged the floor and remained where he was. After the T'aip'ing sat down, he could see, through legs, that T'ang Li was down on the floor, a dagger at his back. The boy thought that it was a case of robbers. At first he decided to remain where he was, then he became afraid that they would find him. He remembered a hole in the wall near the stove. The legs and feet shielded him a good deal and finally he eased back to the wall and along it in the shadow, as silently as a little mouse. He made it to the hole and went through it. Once out, he rose to his feet and ran to get help for T'ang Li.

There were lights in the houses along a street not far away. A street of pleasure for the Japanese soldiers. And by chance, the boy ran headlong into a party of Japanese Intelligence officers, among them Colonel Takara and

Major Shiga. They had been doing a little sightseeing and were all more or less three sheets in the wind.

One of the officers promptly cuffed the boy alongside the ear, at which the boy let out a wail of woe. He began babbling about T'ang Li being robbed and daggers and men sitting on benches, all mixed up.

Colonel Takara, as soon as he heard the name of T'ang Li, said, "Forward, gentlemen. This T'ang Li is a worthy merchant and friendly to Nippon. Take the boy under your arm, Lieutenant Kotito."

As he ran towards the house, it dawned on Takara that if the other officers went in, they might see Chapman and Chapman was very liable to say or do something that would show that he, Takara, had something to do with Chapman's being there.

As they reached the house, Takara said, "Major Shiga and I will go in. The rest of you surround the house. They will run out like rats once they see us. Shoot them down. Come, Major."

Major Shiga drew his revolver with his left hand, came to Takara's side. "It may be—"

"Guard yourselves!" shouted one of the officers, raising his revolver. "We are—" *bang-bang-bang.*

A sudden rush of swordsmen had come from the darkness. Not many swordsmen—five in all. The Jap officers opened fire instantly. Three of the swordsmen went down. The other two reached the Japs. There was a milling around, the Japs trying to avoid the swords and shoot down the Chinese. One officer seized the sword wrist of a Chinese and was shot by a brother officer who could not get his gun out of line quick enough.

"Inside, Major," shouted Takara. "There are—" three of the T'aip'ing came out the door. The fourth, Fang Lu, ran up the stairs to warn the black-eyed smiling one.

THE T'AIP'ING COMING out had no chance. Both Takara and Shiga stood as if at attention and opened fire. The T'aip'ing went down before they got well out of the door-way. And as they did, the two attacking the other officers went down also.

Chapman had just put his feet on the floor when the first shot came. He reached out his hand and grasped the lamp, hurling it straight at Grigsby's head. Grigsby ducked and the lamp hit the wall, broke and set the room on fire. Jimmie Cordie, as the lamp hit the wall, drew his .45 Colt from a shoulder holster and fired at Chapman. But Chapman, as the lamp left his hand, was off balance. He was falling to the right as Jimmie shot. At that, Jimmie almost got him. The bullet took the tip of Chapman's left ear off.

Fang Lu came in, "The little men of Nippon, Lord," he said, calmly. "How many I do not know. Our swords hold them away but for how long I also do not know."

"Out the window," Jimmie commanded. "I guess I got him, George. No time to make sure. You first, Fang Lu."

When Colonel Takara and Major Shiga got to the room they found Chapman, bleeding from the ear, putting out the fire. They helped and between the three of them, got it out.

"Get in that closet," commanded Takara, "and stay there until I release you. Quickly, Mr. Chapman."

"Why the hell should I do that? I'm going to get me a rod and go and get that—"

"You must not be seen here. If you are—we cannot go

through with our plans. Do as I ask—get in the closet. One thousand dollars more for you, if you do so at once."

"Yeah, that's different. Make it snappy, though."

Colonel Takara and Major Shiga were coming down the stairs when Jap officers crowded into the house.

"There are none of the dogs upstairs," Colonel Takara announced. "In some way a fire started. We have put it out. How many of the mongrels were there?"

"We have accounted for eight, Colonel. Four officers are wounded."

"I will get details later. Where is T'ang Li?"

"Here, Colonel."

"Bring him forward. So you were attacked by bandits, T'ang Li?"

"Yes, mighty war lord of Nippon."

11

MAJOR SHIGA IS PERPLEXED

IT TOOK AN hour or more to clear the house of T'ang Li of all save the Chinese leather merchant and Colonel Takara. At last, the colonel felt safe to go up and release Chapman from the closet. He did not know what had happened to Chapman. His first thought had been to see if Chapman had been killed by the robbers. The room was on fire when the two Jap officers rushed in and Colonel Takara had seen that Chapman was bleeding. But that was all he knew.

"What happened?" he demanded, as Chapman went towards a washstand.

"How the hell do I know? I was in bed and the door opened and in came those two— He'll learn me, will he? I wish that—"

"Who came in?"

"That louse named Grigsby and—"

"Grigsby? Came in here? You said two. Who was the other?"

"Some punk called Jimmie. What the hell difference does it make? I'm going to rub that guy from Kentucky out, if it takes me until the second coming." Chapman was holding a wet washrag to his ear.

"Wait a minute, Mr. Chapman. Please sit down and tell me just what happened and what was said."

"Wait till I take a shot. This damn ear hurts like hell. I'll get me a rod and start out for that—" he talked all the time he was taking a big dose of cocaine. Of what he would do to that so and so lad from Kentucky.

Finally, after the drug took hold, he calmed down and Takara got most of what had happened and been said.

"I see. Captain James Cordie and George Grigsby, Big Swords officers and now prisoners of the Badakshan. By any chance, have you told anyone of our plans?"

"No. Who the hell could I tell? I didn't even tell that little kite where I was going."

"That little kite? I do not understand, Mr. Chapman."

"Jee, you Japs are dumb. My wife."

"I am learning rapidly, Mr. Chapman. Then how—you say that—"

"Listen. My wife was a Shelby from Kentucky—get that? This Grigsby is a relation of hers—get that?"

"Yes, Mr. Chapman, I get it."

"All right. Put it down in your book. In some way she must have got to him and squawked about me—how I don't know. You ever heard of Kentucky feuds?"

"Yes, Mr. Chapman. The subject interested me while I was in the States."

"Well, this punk Grigsby hears all about it and he thinks he'll feud me—get it. For what I—what was it he said? Oh, yeah, I got it, because I degraded a Shelby woman. Can you beat that? Yeah—regular Kentucky feud stuff. I'll feud him, the—. And that louse Jimmie also. He took a shot at me and if I hadn't been falling he'd have got me."

"Then, you think that the reason they came was because of—because Grigsby was feuding you?"

"What else?"

"Your wife is still in Vladivostok?"

"How do I know? She was, when I left. She better be there, the little shred."

"Does that also mean wife? How do you think they found out you were here?"

"Aw—how do I know? Scram out of here, will you? I want to sleep."

"I will, Mr. Chapman. I think that to-night it is best to take you to another place. In the meantime, I will see that you are not bothered with, what do you call them? Men from Kentucky who feud?"

"To hell with them. Get me a rod and let 'em all come," Chapman answered from the bed. "Beat it."

COLONEL TAKARA WENT to his quarters where he found Major Shiga waiting for him. He told Shiga what Chapman had told him.

"I can see how they might escape from the Badakshan but—how did they know where the American snake was hidden?" Shiga asked. "And the swordsmen who attacked us were not ordinary Chinese. Do you think it possible that they know of our plan?"

"Impossible, Major. It is as Chapman says. By some chance, simple enough if we knew, they found him. It may be that they went to T'ang Li's shop to get equipment. They did not accuse Chapman of being there to kill Henry Pu-Yi. It was only 'you die for what you have done to a Shelby woman.'"

"That is right, Colonel. Speaking of the swordsmen,

one of the officers told me that he thought they were of the T'aip'ing."

"It may be that they were. Captain Cordie is very close to the T'aip'ing."

"That is news to me. I did not think that any Chinese society ever admitted—"

"I did not say that he was a member, Major Shiga. I said that he was close to them. I understand that once he saved the life of Yen Yuan's only son. Yen Yuan is the 'Head' of the T'aip'ing. Since then they have been at his beck and call. But all this is beside the issue. I take Chapman to-night to a place where all the Big Swords mongrels and the T'aip'ing cannot find him. From there he will be taken to the proper place at the proper time. Supposing you go to the Badakshan camp and see if you can find out how they escaped?"

"I will."

"On the way, arrange for cavalry detachments to comb the hills. It may be that we can pick them up although I doubt it. Captain Cordie is more than clever."

ONCE AGAIN THE line of prisoners sat by the tent. Red Dolan was sounding off. "So, ye think ye missed the scut. How come ye doin' that, Jimmie? Ye never do miss and ye must have been—"

"For Pete's sake! Put a jaw tackle on, you big ape. How can I do any thinking with you wah wahin' all the time. The heck I don't miss, like everyone else. We sure gummed up the parade, George. Misto Jap knows by now that we are out after Chapman. If they have any brains at all they will hook it up and—"

"Why should they?" asked the Bean. "From what you

and George said, there was no mention of anything but the fact that George was going to kill him for what he had done to a Shelby. I don't think they have any idea that we know about what they have framed up to do to Henry."

"Yeah? Maybeso, Codfish. What we should have done is to kill him first and talk to him afterwards. Now the Japs will be on their toes and—"

"What the hell do ye care, Jimmie Cordie? Think up something. The arms ave me are gettin' cramped."

"Do a little thinking yourself, Mr. Dolan."

"Me? Why should I, wid you here?"

"Oi, quite right, Irish bummer. Ain't dot right, Beany?"

"What? Does the likes ave ye sit there and—"

"Listen," Jimmie interrupted. "All I can say is that if you apes don't quit that, we'll sit here until the second coming if you rely on me thinking."

"It is very annoying," the Bean agreed. "The chatter of ring tailed monkeys has always given me the jitters also, Jeems. The only way to keep those so justly called apes quiet is to—"

"Here comes the jolly old Khan with—my word, it's your friend the giddy Major, Beaneater," Carewe interrupted.

"Oi, dis vill be good. I bet you his eyes pop out ven he sees Jimmie und George."

"I wonder if he is hooked up with Takara? Look at old Mangali Boga. He's thinking of the Chi treasure and—" Jimmie switched to Pushtu. "Good morning, mighty Khan of the peerless Badakshan. Have you come to inform us that we have been ransomed?"

The Yid very near called the turn about Major Shiga's eyes popping out. They were, as near as eyes can come to it and not do it. He looked at Jimmie Cordie and at Grigsby as if he did not believe they were really there.

"You see, little man of Nippon?" snarled the Khan. "I had six prisoners yesterday. Count them now. One-two-three-four-five-six. You say you heard that two escaped? Know that prisoners do not escape from the Badakshan. Truly, I am beginning to think that what I have often heard is true."

"Und vot vos it dot you heard, Mistaire—" the Yid began again in Pushtu. "What did you hear, ruler of the world?"

"You dare to speak, Yehuda?" the old Khan spat on the ground. "Silence, dog, or I will start skinning before the relations of those you slew arrive."

Red laughed, "That's tellin' the Hester Street polecat somethin', ye cockeyed old divil. That's what he is, a—"

"You also dare speak, red jackal? Know that you will soon be begging for mercy as the boiling oil creeps higher and higher up your body."

"It is ill," Jimmie Cordie said, gravely, "to revile prisoners, Khan of the Badakshan. You may some time be a prisoner yourself. Why has this little man of Nippon been brought to stare at us?"

"He came and said that he had heard that two of you had escaped. It seemed to worry him greatly, for some unknown reason."

"Escaped? Through ten thousand Badakshan? You flatter us, Major."

"But—but—you were seen. You and Grigsby."

"Some mistake, Major. I am afraid that someone is what we call kidding you."

"I—it may be, Captain Cordie. I have heard that the

effect—" The major stopped talking, a puzzled look in his eyes.

"Go ahead. The effect of what?"

Major Shiga got hold of himself. "The effect of knowing that Big Swords officers are close makes men think things."

"How's your hand?" asked the Bean conversationally.

Major Shiga stared at the Boston Bean for a moment, then answered, smoothly, "I am learning to shoot with my left, hoping against hope that you will escape from the Badakshan."

The Bean laughed, "What 'opes, Major. Tell you what? You help me get away, how's that?"

"Well," growled Mangali Boga, "you have seen them, haven't you? Count them yourself, little man. What do you want now, to stand here and talk to them all day? Truly you of Nippon are fools, all save a few."

MAJOR SHIGA WOULD have dearly loved to tell the old Khan just where he, the Khan, stood in his estimation, but he had too much sense to do it.

"I beg your pardon, mighty leader of the Badakshan. The rumor I heard was false. If it had been true, we of Nippon were going to offer to help retake the dogs for you."

"I can both hold and retake my own prisoners," answered Mangali Boga haughtily. "Come, then."

As Major Shiga and the old Khan walked away, the Yid said, "Did you hear it dot, Jimmie? He can both hold und retake. If he can hold, he would not have to retake, ain't it?"

"I bet you," answered Jimmie, absently. "See if you can hold that trap of yours shut a few minutes, Mr. Cohen."

"Votever de Captain says," answered the Yid, sweetly. Jimmie Cordie had commanded a machine gun company in France and the Yid had been his first sergeant, incidentally that was where he got the name "The Fighting Yid" hung on him.

"He will go back and tell Takara," Jimmie thought out loud, "Takara will think one of two things. Chapman had a snow bird's dream or—old Mangali is playing with us. Then what?"

"And what the hell difference does it make what the little pink toed bamalam thinks?" demanded Red. "Why the hell don't ye think up something and go and get the cokey? Are ye goin' to let him kick the gong around and crack down on—"

"Vate—red jackal dot you are. A cokey sniffs it cocaine. Only von dot smokes it opium kicks de gong around. Come to Poppa ven you—" The Yid only got that far because Red was drawing a long breath.

"So—ye know all about it, ye—ye—" Red spat in imitation of Mangali Boga. "Ye Yehuda! And a bad wan ye are. All the Cohens are Yehudas. Some ave them worse than—Jimmie, what the hell is a Yehuda?"

"What? What the heck are you talking about, Red?"

"I'm callin' the Yid a Yehuda. What is it? 'Tis what the old divil called him."

"My gosh! How the heck can anyone do any figuring with you around. A Yehuda is a Jew, you nitwit."

"Is that all? I thought that—"

"Supposing you and the Yid and the Bean go back of the tent. You don't seem to realize that to even attempt to do what we came here to do and get away from the Japs takes anything more than a lot of kidding. Go back of the tent and kid about the rope that is darn near your necks."

"Have I lived to see the day that ye, Jimmie Cordie ave the Legion, say that—"

"You have. If we—here comes Fang Lu. Come on, George and Carewe. We'll get back of the tent with him."

"Don't do 'er, Jimmie darlin'. I'm shut," Red protested.

"Und so am I, no foolink," the Yid said, hastily. He always wanted to know all about everything.

"I am deeply grieved and pained, Jeems, me good man," the Bean mourned, "that you class me with these two unspeakable morons. But as long as you do, I also am shut—no foolink."

Jimmie laughed, "I love you all—like a burglar loves a cop. Stick around—fizzledicks."

12

SECRET TUNNEL

FANG LU DID not have anything special to report. He came more to make sure that Jimmie Cordie and Grigsby were once more set in the Badakshan lines. The night, or rather the morning before, they had become separated. Jimmie ordered that all the T'aip'ing within reach were to be concentrated and that watch was to be kept on the house of T'ang Li and also that Colonel Takara and Major Shiga were to be covered. His idea was that by a sudden attack in force, Chapman could be reached, and afterwards a way cut to the hills before the Japs recovered from the surprise. Fang Lu had told him that he, Fang Lu, thought that all in all, there were some two hundred T'aip'ing within a radius of a hundred miles. Jimmie knew that the Japs would not let any small party, no matter what the party posed as, get within striking distance of Chapman again. Jimmie was sure that he had missed Chapman, the sixth sense of a marksman told him that.

Fang Lu said that it would take two or three days to get the T'aip'ing together and Jimmie, feeling that it was the only thing to do, ordered all possible haste to be made. Fang Lu agreed.

The Japs seemed to have forgotten all about the Big

Swords prisoners the next few days. Red, the Bean and
the Yid passed the time having regular Kilkenny cat argu-
ments, sometimes a three cornered affair, other times two
against one. Carewe, Jimmie Cordie and Grigsby talked
of Big Swords affairs and of other campaigns, keeping as
far away from the three arguers as possible.

The fourth morning, Fang Lu came back. The T'aip'ing,
two hundred odd, were ready for the orders of the "black
eyed smiling one "but—Colonel Takara and Chapman
had disappeared.

"Disappeared?" Jimmie asked. "With the eyes of the
T'aip'ing on them?"

"The man of Nippon was seen going into the shop
of T'ang Li. The one there did not come out. Our eyes
cannot see through walls, elder brother."

"That is right, little brother. And then?"

"Neither has the man of Nippon come out. Last night,
one of those who watched, while the merchant and the
youth were away, entered the shop. Neither the one you
are after or the man of Nippon were there."

"Holy cats! A tunnel. They have taken him to another
place. Well—he has got to be found, Fang Lu. Scatter the
T'aip'ing out and hunt for him. Wait. To-night I go with
you. My war brothers will remain here."

There was much objection from Red when Jimmie
told what he was going to do. That he was going out with
the T'aip'ing and staying out until Chapman was found.
Grigsby did not like it, but at last admitted that Jimmie
Cordie could do no more than that, and under the circumstances it would be foolish to have two go.

"I'll attend to the feudin' for you, George," Jimmie said

with a grin. "Come to think of it my great, great grandma was a Shelly. I bet you the real name was Shelby.

"You bamalams couldn't catch the measles. Stick around. Pretty soon I'll come dancing in barefooted with the bad old killer's head on a silver platter."

"Ye are more apt to be dancin' barefooted on nawthin'," answered Red, pessimistically. At which the hard-bitted, reckless adventurers all laughed.

But Jimmie Cordie did no dancing, either with a silver platter or on thin air. Search as the T'aip'ing could and did, with all their power and skill brought into play, they could find no trace either of Colonel Takara or of Chapman. Two of them got T'ang Li out in the open one night and what they did to that Chinese spy was, as the Yid would say, "plenty und den some." He admitted that there was a tunnel and that it led to a house in San-sing's business district. He also admitted that Colonel Takara and Chapman had gone down in the tunnel. Where they had gone he did not know. Finally the T'aip'ing agreed that T'ang Li did not know—which was a great relief for T'ang Li. They took him to a place where he would be incommunicado for as long as desired and told him as they left that if he opened his mouth about what had happened to him, he and his relations to the ninth degree would deeply regret his talkativeness. T'ang Li assured them, between groans, that all the Li were first cousins to the clam family.

What the T'aip'ing got out of T'ang Li did not do Jimmie Cordie any good. The trouble was that the Japs might have Chapman in San-sing, Shuntien, Hsinking or three or four other places within striking distance of the Altar or the line of march to it.

It was dangerous hunting, the slightest break meaning death for Jimmie Cordie. He was made up more than
cleverly as a Chinese coolie and there were always several
others that surrounded him but—the danger was there.
And there was no delaying the ceremony that spelled trag-
edy.

13

JIMMIE'S SECRET

AT LAST, A break came for Jimmie Cordie. It did not look like one and it maybe should not be called one. A better way to put it would be that it started lifting the seeming impregnable fog.

A T'aip'ing reported to Jimmie and Fang Lu that an old Manchu woman told him that a day or so ago she had sold to a Japanese officer a drug that makes the person taking it like a child—an obedient little child.

"We have been hunting in the wrong fields, little brothers," Jimmie Cordie said. "Now we will hunt along the line of march to the Altar and around it. Find any and all places where a rifleman might be concealed whose rifle commands the Altar or the way to it. There are not many houses. Find out who lives in the house and what they do. Find out if any space has been rented and to whom. We will start searching for a place."

"It will not be hard to find, honorable elder brother. All that live along the road are Chinese. There is no house near the Altar itself."

"That makes it easier. Start from where Henry Pu-Yi leaves his palace. I go back now to the Badakshan camp and await you, Fang Lu. First, buy and bring to me some of the drug that makes one like a little child."

"As you order, mighty honorable elder brother of the resplendent Head."

LIEUTENANT-GENERAL NAGAYO WAS a pleasure loving gentleman and when not on duty gratified his desires as far as he could. The night before the Emperor, Henry Pu-Yi, was due to parade to the Altar and there make his peace with Heaven, Nagayo had indulged in a little stepping out. He did not want it known generally that he was doing it, so he had arranged matters so that he could slip into a place where wine, women, and song awaited him, without any of the Jap officers knowing about it, except a young captain of his staff. He had his good time and in the wee small hours left the place and sauntered along towards the place where the young captain was waiting for him. That he could be in any danger never occurred to him. He was about in the center of a Japanese division and there was no reason why he should not unbelt.

He passed a cart from which the horses had been taken. Just as he cleared it, something hit him on the head. If Nagayo had time to think of anything he must have thought the heavens had fallen in.

When he finally came back to life he was sitting propped up on a couch and there were three Chinese standing in front of him. He stared at them and finally said, "What does this mean? You pariah curs will die many deaths for—" Jimmie Cordie, still in disguise but with the coolie hat off, stepped up where Nagayo could see him.

"What's the matter, General?"

"You! You are responsible for this outrage? By all the Gods, Captain Cordie, you will pay for this. You dare—"

"Something seems to have got you all fussed up, General. When you were a lowly colonel you were much more calm and collected."

"You must be crazy, you Yankee mongrel. My absence will be noted and—"

"I'll send word to Headquarters that you are busy on Intelligence work, General. All right, Fang Lu."

A little later Jimmie said, "Well, that's that. Take care of him, little brother."

"LISTEN TO ME, Jimmie Cordie," Red commanded, firmly. "Ye have something up the sleeve ave ye, don't tell me different. Ye sit here wid a grin on the face ave ye, doin' nawthin and 'tis well ye know that tomorrow the Manchu scut goes to the Altar. Ye said so yeself last night. Ye have not found Chapman, ye have done nawthin and yet, ye sit and grin."

"Well, what the heck do you want me to do, run around crying? I've done the best I could, please sir. All I can think of now is what the Japs are going to do with us when old Mangali Boga gives us up."

"Go on, ye can't fool me, who has been wid ye for many the year. Ye are not the wan to sit grinnin', me bucko. Tell me, Jimmie, darlin'."

"Go ahead, redhead, smooch it out of him. He is holdin' out on us."

"Who asked ye to butt in, ye dish faced scut? Jimmie is not. He wouldn't do such a thing, would ye, Jimmie alanna?"

"Heck I wouldn't, ye big ape. You and the Yid and the

Bean, a fine three to draw to. Who kidded the Japs when I said not to?"

"Again I am wrongfully associated with the lower classes," the Bean objected. "I did not kid the Japs, Jeems. Tell me. Remember that time when the Bat d'Af gang tried to clean up on us at Abibad? Who stood at your back and fought them offen you? While Red ran as fast as he could? None other but yours truly, John—"

"The while I ran? I never ran in me life, ye Bosting beaneater. If the hands ave me was untied, I'd cram that lie down the throat ave ye."

"Tell you vot," suggested the Yid. "Ve get it Red und de Bean untied und let dem go to it. It vill pass avay de time und—"

"Get yerself untied also, me bully. After I take the Codfisher apart I'll do the same for ye."

"Sic 'em, Red. I'm for you. I got ten dollars that says you can do it."

"Wait a minute," the Bean protested. "Can't you two nuts see that Jeems is sidetracking us? Are you going to tell us, Jeems?"

"No, I am not."

"Sorry the day. Sorry the day indeed that I live to hear Jimmie Cordie says he won't tell us somethin'. For years we have fought by the side ave him in the cold and in the hot. Wounded we have been and wounded he has been and always we have been—"

"Sure I will tell you anything I know, you big redheaded fool."

"Oh, ye will? That's different, ye black muzzled scut.

I knew ye would all the time. Go ahead, Jimmie darlin'.
What have ye up the sleeve ave ye?"

"I have my arm up my sleeve. Listen, we gave up hunting for Chapman and hunted instead for the place he is to
be planted to get Henry Pu-Yi. We found it and for Pete's
sake don't ask me how, either. We know exactly where he
is going to be placed, at what window and everything. We
are going to try and stop him firing on Henry. We—"

"Who the hell is we?" interrupted Red.

"Me and the T'aip'ing," answered Jimmie with a grin.

"Oh, ye are? Ye and the T'aip'ing. And what are we
supposed to do, sit here and suck the thumbs ave us?"

"My good man, how can you suck your thumbs when
they are both tied behind your back?" asked the Bean, in
a bored tone.

"Vot, don't you know, Beany? De red jackal is von of
dem tvisters. You know, vot turns it demselves inside out?"

"You mean a turncoat? I thought that only the black
Irish were turncoats?"

"Ye have gone too far, Beaneater," Red said, bitterly, "ye
have gone too far. The Yid gibbon I pay no attention to,
but ye—listen to me, ye—"

Red forgot all about pressing Jimmie for further elabora-
tion of what Jimmie had up his sleeve besides his arm. And
before he and the Yid, who joined in with Red against the
Bean, and the Bean got through, Jimmie Cordie, George
Grigsby and Carewe disappeared, one by one.

Red, when he tired of blackguarding the Bean, looked
around. "What the hell! Where's Jimmie?"

"Und George und Carewe?"

The Bean laughed. "Evidently we are not included in what Jimmie had up his sleeve."

"The dirty ditchers! Come on, we'll get these ropes untied and go and—"

"Vate a minute, Red. If Jimmie vanted us along he vould have taken us. He vants us right here for some reason. Maybe if ve vent, it vould fog him up."

"Why didn't he tells us, then? 'Tis the first time he ever—"

"It may be well, me good man," the Bean interrupted mildly, "that we did not give him a chance. He started to tell us and you began sounding off as usual."

"Right ye are, Beany, for a wonder. 'Tis our own fault."

"Vy say it 'our,' Irish gonif? Dot's vot ve get, Codfisher, for beink friends mit a Irisher."

"You are quite correct, Mr. Cohen. From now on I am intirely offen all Irishers and redheaded ones in particular."

Red's answer consigned the Yid and the Bean to a place where no one wishes to go and also included a description of their ancestors.

14

THE FAKE DUEL

SEVERAL JAPANESE NON-COMMISSIONED officers were on their way to secure a good place to see the ceremony at the Altar. One of them was being kidded by the others. Army kidding is not at all delicate and the non-com on the receiving end was getting more and more angry. It seems that he had bought a watch from a Chinese peddler. The case was supposed to be gold and the Jap had paid a good price for it. Not only had the watch stopped running but the case had begun to turn green. Instead of keeping still about it, the young non-com had broadcasted his sorrow at being done in. As a result, he was made the butt of many more or less witty remarks that occurred to his buddies.

"Wait," he declared, "I will find that dog of a Chinese and make him not only give me my money back but also—"

"How will you know him when you see him?" asked a corporal. "You cannot even tell when a watch case is only washed with gold."

"I will make the first one of them I see repay me. He can collect from the one who—who—look, here comes some of them. Now I will show you whether I am a fool or not."

The Tartars have a saying, "Erein mor nigen bui," which

in English is, "A man's path is only one." In other words, "Thy fate is written upon thy forehead and alter it thou canst not."

However true the above is fate, or what you will, placed the Japanese non-commissioned officers squarely in the path of Jimmie Cordie, Grigsby and Carewe, all made up as Chinese peddlers. With them were six of the T'aip'ing.

"Spread out a little," an older non-com commanded. "Let them think they are passing between us. Then Oama can—"

"I have a better plan," another interrupted. "We will take them all to Captain Saigo's machine gun company. He and the lieutenants are away and First Sergeant Taira is a friend of mine. We will claim that some one of them robbed a private of our regiment. Taira will hold them for us until after the ceremony. Then we will take them some other place and"—he grinned—"relieve them of their burdens."

"That is a fine plan. We will all share alike—after Oama collects for his watch. Here, officers might come along."

The Japanese spread out and the real and synthetic Chinese, heads down, started to scuttle through them. Suddenly a non-com drew his revolver and commanded, "Halt."

The peddlers halted, that was all they could do. There was absolutely no chance to make a break. Other Japanese were fairly close and all wore their side arms.

As they halted, the T'aip'ing got around the soldiers of fortune. "Will we cut the way for you, honorable elder brother?" the leader asked, softly.

"No," answered Jimmie, "it may be that—pretend to be afraid and do as they command until—"

The Japs formed a line and the one with the drawn revolver commanded, "Forward!"

A T'aip'ing began, "But why, mighty warrior? We have permission to—"

"Silence, pariah cur. Forward."

Other revolvers appeared in the hands of the non-coms in the line as the command was issued. Again there was nothing to do but obey, either that or die right there. The life of a Chinese was considered worth less than nothing and Jimmie Cordie and the others knew it. The soldiers would trump up some story of being attacked—afterwards.

They were marched to where a machine gun company was stationed. One of the units placed by the Japanese in strategical positions all around the city. The first sergeant came forward and after a moment's conversation, walked up to the peddlers and snarled, "Get over there near those boxes and stay there."

For the third time, a command was obeyed. Not all the company was with the machine guns. Quite a few had leave to see the ceremony but there were plenty left to stop any running away. The Jap non-coms laughed and swaggered away, very sure that right after they saw Henry Pu-Yi go through the ceremony at the Altar they would be dividing the contents of nine trays of goods and also what money the peddlers had on them.

THE JAPS OF the company paid no attention to the group, more than a curious look or two. The first sergeant shouted, "Go on with your work." And as he was greatly feared by the men of the company, they obeyed.

"My word," Carewe said, "what a giddy old mess, what,

what, what? I say, Jimmie, this will take some quick think-ing."

"It will take more than thinking, Jonathan, old kid. The Nine Red Gods are playing against us. In less than an hour, Henry Pu-Yi starts for the Altar. If the Intelligence had caught us I wouldn't feel so darn washed out. But having a bunch of Jap non-coms pick us up for some unknown reason just at the wrong moment, gets my well known goat. If they had only taken one more drink of rice wine before they started for the parade, we would have been in the clear."

"That 'if' is a sad word, Jimmie," Grigsby said. "You can 'if' yourself all the way back to when the world was created. If this had not happened, that wouldn't. Let's see what we can do. If—there I go 'if-ing' myself. Anyway, if one of us could reach those houses, he could go through with it."

Jimmie turned a little and looked over at the rear of several Chinese shacks that were within two hundred feet. "That's right, George. But they might just as well be at the North Pole. Two hundred odd feet to go in the open with fifty or sixty Japs who would rather crack down on us than not."

"I say! If we could think of something that would attract their jolly old attention for a few seconds, one of us might make it."

Jimmie Cordie laughed, not a very happy laugh, either. He was seeing, in his mind's eye, Henry Pu-Yi go down under a bullet fired by an American and thinking of what would happen afterwards. He had been so cocksure that he was going to prevent it and now—he was sitting about in the middle of a Jap machine gun company and the

minutes were ticking off. "Go ahead and think of something. Darned if I can."

One of the T'aip'ing who could understand and speak
quite a little English, said, "We will charge the little
mongrels, black eyed smiling one. There are six of us and
we have our swords. In the confusion, you, our elder blothels, can lun."

"There are not any of them near enough to you. See how
they are scattered out. Before you could reach them with
your good swords, they would have drawn their guns, little
brother. The guns would speak fast and—and—if we could
bunch them in some way—little brother, you are ready
always to die for the society?"

"Yes, mighty one honoled by the all powelful Head.
Tluly, what better death could be found? To die, swold
in hand, for the T'aip'ing, means that our lelations to the
ninth delgee will be enliched and honoled. We seek always
the chance."

"That I know—is true. Because in doing it I may save
the lives of countless men and also the lives of women and
gentle little ones—I, the honorable elder brother of the
resplendent Head, send you to your death, little brothers."

"Give oldels."

"Four of you rise and begin to talk very angrily, two
against two. After the count of ten, one will strike another
in the face with the hand. Then all four become calm and
back away from each other a little ways. I mean two back
away from the other two. Is that plain?"

"Yes, elder blother, it is plain."

"Then, one who remains seated jumps up and calls to
the Nippon sergeant who stands there by the gun. When

he comes up he will be told that the four wish to fight a sword duel. If he agrees, fight the duel. It may be that the men of Nippon will crowd around to see it. If they do, they will push us, who remain here out of their way. It may be that we can make the houses. If they see us trying, those that fight and the two who watch will close with them and—take their attention for as long as possible. It will be to the death, little brother, unless we make it to the houses without being seen. If we do, stop the duel after you have fought long enough to make it look real. The little men of Nippon will think that three of the peddlers have escaped through no fault of yours. Are you ready?"

"Yes, honolable elder blother, as soon as I tell those who cannot undelstand English."

The Jap non-com looked over as four of the Chinese jumped up and began an excited, shrill argument. He made no move to come over, probably thinking it just a squabble between peddlers. But when one of those who remained seated rose and called to him, he sauntered over.

"What is it?" he rasped. He was told that the four who argued wanted to fight a duel. "What with? Those pocket knives in that tray?"

"No, they have swords, General."

"Oh, they have, have they? Chinese with swords concealed under their robes. It is against orders and—" the sergeant stopped talking for a moment. He was angry because he could not see the ceremony and also very much bored. Let the Chinese fight and afterwards he could find out from the survivors why swords were being carried. The fact that he had promised to hold them for the other non-coms didn't make any difference to him. Let them guard their own prisoners if they wanted to keep them.

"All right," he went on, "let them fight." Then he thought he would let the men of the company in on it and afterwards make them pay him for the show. He shouted, "A duel is to be fought! Come and see it!"

AS HE SHOUTED, the T'aip'ing drew their swords from under their blouses and began circling each other, two against two. The Japanese soldiers, nothing loath, ran in from all sides. What Jimmie hoped for, came true. He, Grigsby, Carewe and the two remaining T'aip'ing were pushed, kicked and rolled out of the way and the Japs formed a circle around the contestants.

"Let's go, Jimmie," Grigsby said, as he picked himself up.

"I'm on my way," Jimmie answered, with a grin, as he got on his feet. "All right, Carewe?"

"Right, Jimmie."

They started, the two T'aip'ing with them. And right after they did, a little Jap who had been pushed out of the circle, saw them. He yelled something and two or three others who were also on the outside, turned and looked. They all reached for their revolvers. The two T'aip'ing turned and, drawing their swords, charged straight at the Japs. It was their last charge and they knew it. The Japs opened fire, naturally not at the three running figures but at the two men who were coming sword in hand. Some of the Japs missed and some hit. But two T'aip'ing got to them. One Jap went down, then another. A third reeled back, his right arm hanging by a shred. A fourth went down and then down went the T'aip'ing. They had gained for their relations to the ninth degree much honor and riches.

THE FOUR DUELISTS, as the shots rang out, stopped
fighting each other, came into a line, and charged the Japanese making the circle. It was six or seven men deep where
the T'aip'ing hit it, about on a line with where the shots
came from. They were swordsmen all and all, now that the
chance had come to die for the society, absolutely berserk.
The front row Japs fought back as much as they could and
no one could blame them for doing it. Their revolvers were
in the holsters and a sword charge is not a pleasant thing
to face barehanded. In fact there are few worse things to
face, as anyone knows who has ever faced one.

The Japs around the circle in other places could not fire
for fear of hitting their own men. The T'aip'ing cut their
way almost through the circle before they went down and
in doing it, gave the Japs plenty to think about besides
three fleeing peddlers. The Japs on the outside who had
seen the three forgot all about them as they, the Japs, tried
to get in to help their comrades down what appeared to be
four madmen with swords.

Jimmie Cordie, Grigsby and Carewe made it to the
back of one of the houses and crashed through a door into
a kitchen. Sitting at a table were two Japanese officers, a
bottle and glasses at their hands. They had dropped in to
have a quiet drink before going to the ceremony. Jimmie
Cordie very seldom cursed but as he saw them, this time
he did. "Well! What the hell, now?"

The Japs, as the door came in, both rose and their hands
went to their revolver butts. They had no way of knowing
that what looked like one big Chinese and two smaller ones
were three of the most famous Big Swords officers. They

had heard the shots, but had thought that some tribesmen were celebrating the ceremony a little in advance.

If they had known they would have drawn and fired; as it was, they hesitated for a split second. The hesitation cost them promotion and also a few days in the hospital.

George Grigsby reached them first. He uppercutted the one on his right and the little Jap literally sailed through the air to hit the wall, out long before his head made contact. Jimmie Cordie sent a straight left for the other Jap's chin but it was ducked. The Jap started to draw but his revolver had not come more than an inch out of the holster before Grigsby got him. He was lifted up and slammed down on the floor so hard that the next thing he knew was that he was in a hospital bed.

There was an old Chinese in the kitchen who had been waiting on the Japs. He was crouching in a corner, fully expecting to be killed. Jimmie Cordie went over to him and jerked him to his feet. "Which way out?"

The old Chinese shook his head and whimpered like a badly scared child. "You might try Chinese, Jimmie," Grigsby said, calmly.

Jimmie Cordie laughed. "We'll try to find the way without his help." He let go the old man, who sank to the floor, thankful that in some miraculous way his life had been spared. They ran through a door that opened into a hall, to find the hall did not lead anywhere except to other rooms. Back to the kitchen they went and out of it through another door. This time they got into a hall that led through the house to the front door. "Listen," Jimmie said, as he opened the door, "there goes the music—we are too late."

"We may not be, Jimmie. Walk out as if we had been

visiting and now on our way to see the parade," Grigsby
answered.

15

PARADE TO THE ALTAR

THE ALTAR OF Heaven, built at Shuntien, five miles from the capital, Hsinking, is about twenty-five feet wide at the base and fifteen at the top. The steps were covered with the Imperial Yellow and on the steps were red lacquered tables on which rested golden dragons.

The actual ceremony was screened from all eyes but those of eleven Manchus of the Blood. But the parade to the Altar could be seen by all that wished to see it. First, Japanese infantry, cavalry, and artillery. Then Manchu nobles who were for the Japanese. Then Henry Pu-Yi, "Emperor Kang Teh," marching alone. He wore a yellow robe embroidered in golden orchids and jade dragons. Then more Manchus and Japanese officials, staff officers, civilians, and so on. Other branches of the service.

Henry Pu-Yi was a shining mark for anyone who was at all a shot with a rifle. In a house along the line of march, on the second floor, there was a room whose window commanded a close view of the whole affair save what went on behind the screens at the Altar.

When the parade started, the room was empty. As Henry Pu-Yi got to within a thousand feet of the house, the door of the room opened. Colonel Takara entered with Chapman. In Chapman's right hand was a .30-30 American rifle which Takara had procured in some way. The American's eyes and face were calm and untroubled looking. He was a killer, working at his trade, that was all. Takara had not found it necessary to give Chapman the drug that would make him like a child. The Japanese Intelligence officer found that all that was required was that Chapman be given enough cocaine.

"Go to the window," Takara commanded. "Keep out of sight as much as possible. He will have on a yellow robe and be walking alone. When he gets within—"

"Scram, punk. I know what to do. He's just the same as dead, right now."

"That is right, Mr. Chapman. After you—make him quite dead, leave the room and go into the hall. Go down the hall to the last door on your left. Open the door and go in. There will be a man there who will take care of your— what do you call it? Oh, yes, your getaway."

"All right. Beat it. I see him comin'. This is too easy."

Takara left the room as Chapman knelt by the window after cocking the rifle.

He heard the door close after Takara but he did not hear a section of the wall slip noiselessly back. Jimmie Cordie, Grigsby and Carewe had been in time.

George Grigsby entered the room in his stocking feet. He eased up to Chapman as quietly as a leopard sneaks up on its prey. An arm went around Chapman's neck and tightened. Another arm went around Chapman's waist, lifting him up. It was as if Chapman was caught in the coils of a great boa-constrictor. He could not call out, neither could he move save for the threshing around of arms and legs.

GRIGSBY CARRIED HIM to the opening made in the wall and through it. A moment later Jimmie Cordie came through the opening with Lieutenant-General Nagayo, who was as a little obedient child. He had been given the same kind of drug Takara thought it unnecessary to use on Chapman.

Jimmie Cordie carried a .30-30 rifle. "Come to the window," he said. "Now, kneel down. See, here is a rifle. It is cocked, so be careful. Soon will come soldiers, then a man marching alone. He will have on a yellow robe on which are flowers. You will aim the rifle at this man and fire it. Be very sure to hit him with the bullet. He is a bad man and must be killed. Do you understand? You must fire at this man and kill him."

"Yes, I understand. He is a bad man and I must fire the rifle at him."

"That is right, little one. You will get candy and whatever you wish if you do it well. I am going out now but I will come back as soon as you kill the bad man."

"I will kill the bad man."

"That is a good boy."

Jimmie Cordie handed Nagayo the rifle, which was loaded with blanks and went back through the opening, leaving Lieutenant-General Nagayo kneeling where Chapman had knelt.

As he did, the Jap soldiers were passing the house. There were many Chinese and Japanese civilians, men, women, tribesmen, and nondescripts watching the parade as well as Jap soldiers. They were crowded against the houses on either side as there were no sidewalks.

In front of the house where Nagayo knelt at the window stood Major Shiga and the staff captain who had been waiting for Lieutenant-General Nagayo the night Nagayo had been hit on the head. He had been very discreetly looking for Nagayo and thinking that at last Nagayo had slipped up and got so drunk he had forgotten all about the ceremony.

"Let's go, Jimmie," Grigsby said, as Fang Lu put the section of wall back in place. Grigsby and Carewe were holding Chapman down on the floor. The killer had ceased to struggle and lay as if unconscious. In the floor of the room was a trap door.

"Go? With the curtain up for the last act? I should say not. Take your boy friend and go down the ladder if you don't want to stay."

Grigsby laughed. "I'll stick around. It won't be—listen to the shouts."

"He must be coming. Choke that rat down and come to a slit. It'll be worth seeing, George."

"Go ahead, George," Carewe said, "I'll see to it that this rotter keeps still. I think he is already choked down."

Jimmie Cordie and Grigsby, looking through two slits cut in the wall, saw Lieutenant-General Nagayo reach for the rifle, put it to his shoulder, aim and fire it.

It seemed to be a split second afterwards that Colonel Takara and Major Shiga crashed into the room. It was longer, of course, but to Jimmie Cordie and Grigsby the crack of the rifle and the entrance of the two Jap officers

Nagayo snarled, "You pariah curs will die many deaths for—"

almost came together. Right behind them came the staff captain and several other officers and Japanese officials.

As Takara and Shiga cleared the door, Nagayo was getting up on his feet, his back turned to them. They both had revolvers in their hands and they both emptied them into Nagayo's back.

"Here he is," shouted Takara, "we—oh!"

Nagayo had fallen against the window sill, then turned a little, before he crumpled to the floor. He was dead before he turned.

Every Japanese in the room stood as if paralyzed. Lieutenant-General Nagayo! Killed in an attempt to assassinate Henry Pu-Yi! It was unbelievable and yet—there lay his body.

"I—we—it is a—" Major Shiga stammered. "We thought he was—"

JUST THEN, CHAPMAN yelled, "Help! Help! In here! I—" Carewe tried to shut him off. He threw Carewe off and in doing it, felt and got Carewe's gun. Jimmie Cordie and Grigsby turned from the slits as Chapman got on his feet, Carewe's Colt .45 in hand. The Jap officers had snapped out of it and were trying to break the wall down. Others had run out of the room and were hunting for the door leading into the room the yells had come from. By chance, more than anything else, the door was not on the hall-way. The room opened into another which in turn opened into a third that was reached by a little independent hall branching out from the main hall. Chinese houses are oddly constructed from an Occidental standard.

"Now," Chapman snarled, "I'll show you punks some shooting."

Grigsby laughed, "Show it to me." As he turned from the slit, Grigsby had drawn his Colt .45.

Chapman, while speaking, was raising Carewe's gun. He should not have done that. Not when he was to shoot it out with one of the fastest and best shots in the Orient. George Grigsby put three bullets into Chapman while Chapman was pulling trigger. The bullet hit Grigsby in the shoulder. Grigsby's bullets tore through Chapman's heart, all three of them.

"Did he get you?" Jimmie asked, as the dead body of Chapman went to the floor.

"In the shoulder. Get going, Jimmie. I'll hold them until—"

"Behave. Fang Lu, get that body down the ladder. Give George a hand, Carewe. Make it snappy, gents. Old man Cordie's son, Jimmie, will play Horatius at the bridge."

"Come along, Jimmie—or Carewe and I stay."

"If that's the case, I will. No use of—here they come!"

Fang Lu had already disappeared with Chapman's body. Grigsby and Carewe were at the trap door, Grigsby on the ladder, when Japanese officers crowded into the room, or rather in the doorway. Jimmie Cordie fired at them. The front officers, two of them, went down and the others, behind, recoiled for a moment. There was a moment's confusion and delay among the Japanese. Jimmie Cordie got to the ladder and on it before two officers jumped over the two whom had fallen. They both fired at Jimmie and both missed. It may have been because Jimmie hit both of them as they jumped. Before two more could get in, Jimmie Cordie was far enough down the ladder to reach up and close, also lock with a heavy bar, the trap door.

The T'aip'ing had suddenly appeared through a hole in the kitchen of the house early that morning. The house owner, in Takara's pay, needed only a sword flashed before his eyes and a rasped threat of T'aip'ing wrath, to make him forget all about Japanese officers. He had plenty of loved relations scattered all over China and knew what the T'aip'ing would do to them, to the ninth degree of kinship. He told of the sliding section of wall, which most Chinese houses have. The trap door was cut long before Takara appeared with Chapman from a cell-like little room on the ground floor. He had chosen the room because it was secluded from the rest of the house. It was so secluded that anyone in it could not hear what was going on in the rest of the house.

THE JAPANESE OFFICERS tried for a minute or two, to open the trap door but could not. Colonel Takara came in. "No use, gentlemen. They are well away by now. It is the

Yankee mongrels who pose as prisoners of the Badakshan. They placed Lieutenant-General Nagayo there and—"

"That is right," a young officer interrupted. "We will take them from the Badakshan and make them tell—"

"Wait," commanded a high ranking officer. "How did Lieutenant-General Nagayo fall in their hands? There is something very strange about this matter, gentlemen. We cannot afford to have it made public. No matter what we make the Yankee dogs say under torture, the world will think that we planned to assassinate Henry Pu-Yi and in some way failed. We had much better report to Headquarters and let the Staff handle it."

"That—is true," Takara answered, slowly. "It must be hushed up—as far as the killing of Lieutenant-General Nagayo is concerned. But as far as the Big Swords are concerned, the time has come to wipe them out, once for all. We know that they are responsible for this."

"We will swear that we saw them—I have it. They were here to assassinate Henry Pu-Yi. Lieutenant-General Nagayo found it out and came to prevent them doing it. He was formerly of the Intelligence and so—his presence is explained. They killed him and—" The staff captain stopped talking as the ranking officer shook his head.

"How can we swear that on our honor? I for one, will not. No—let us tell the truth. The High Command will then do as they see fit. What we can do is to hide the body of Lieutenant-General Nagayo and leave officers here to see to it that none but us know who it was that was slain."

"Let us go, then," Takara answered. "I, for one, will not rest or eat until the Big Swords curs have paid in full for what they have done."

Headquarters, after hearing what had happened, promptly ordered every officer who knew anything about it to forget the entire matter. Nagayo's body was removed under cover of the darkness that night and the next day it was given out that he had died suddenly during the night.

And at the same time, orders were issued that the Big Swords prisoners were to be taken from the Badakshan, by force if necessary. No reasons were to be given. They were to be taken, that is all. Officers were detailed to go to Mangali Boga and demand the prisoners. Troops were moved up close and if he refused to give them up, the Badakshan were to be shot if they resisted, future relations with tribes or no future relations. The Japs had more than they wanted from the soldiers of fortune who fought for the Big Swords and were going to make an end to it.

16

A DUEL TO DEATH

"SO," MANGALI BOGA said, "the trick is played."

"Yes," Jimmie Cordie answered, "it is played."

"Now what?"

"Soon the little men of Nippon will come and demand that you surrender us."

"Let them demand. Am I a child to be treated as such? Let them demand. I am Mangali Boga of the Badakshan."

"That's right. But even you cannot withstand the might of the little men. We escape, Mangali Boga. Horses are ready for us back of your lines. How we did it you do not know. All you do know is that—we are gone. It may be that we bribed some of the guards. If we did, you know nothing of it."

"I will handle the little men of Nippon. I am released?"

"Yes, you are released. Come to the treasure house of Chi whenever you please."

"It will be soon. I will be very angry at the little men of Nippon and withdraw to the hills, saying I will not fight for them. Once there, I will go to the treasure house of Chi."

"All right. We haven't much time. Good bye, Mangali Boga. You have kept your word and the House of Chi will do the same."

"I know that, blood brother of Sahet Khan. Good bye."

Jimmie Cordie ran to the tent, "Let's go."

"Where?" demanded Red. "So, ye sneaked out on us, did ye? And now ye come up and say, 'Let's go,' as if ye—go where and how?"

"On horses, Mr. Dolan. Where, to the Big Swords. How is your shoulder, George?"

"I can ride, Jimmie."

"Fine. We've got some to do."

"Where are the horses?" asked Red. "How long can these little scuts ave hill ponies hold us up? 'Tis big men we are and—"

"They are not ponies, Mr. Dolan, they are regular race horses donated to us by some friends of mine. Think of a few more questions to ask and your bamalam friends will be here to answer them for you. Come on."

As the Yid mounted, he said to the Bean, "I vunder how dey did it. Do you know, Codfisher?"

"How the hell and high water could I know? Get over a little."

Red rode up beside Jimmie, "Jimmie darlin', what came off? George and Carewe didn't tell us much."

"Well, we got Chapman, that's one thing. The Japs framed it to have him kill Henry Pu-Yi and—"

"I know that much."

"Yeah? Do some riding, then, and quit asking me questions."

"Tell me, Jimmie. I don't know nawthin."

"I thought you just said you did? We got hold of Lieutenant-General Nagayo and substituted him for Chapman.

The Japs killed him, thinking he was Chapman. Now you know all about it."

"Mary Mother! Jimmie, did ye know he would be killed?"

"I did not. I thought they would come busting in, see him instead of Chapman and all run around in circles."

Red rode without saying anything for a moment, then, "Would ye have put him there if ye knew he was going to get killed, Jimmie?"

"No one knows what he will do under given circumstances, Mr. Dolan."

"I guess that's right. How did ye find Chapman?"

"The T'aip'ing found him."

"I mean, how did ye find the place?"

"The T'aip'ing found that, too. Then they bought the house next door and tunneled over."

"How did ye make the scut ave a Nagayo come through for ye?"

"You probably know about the drug named Shenli which makes the person taking it like a good nine year old kid. The T'aip'ing got us some and we fed it to Nagayo. Then we hid him away until—here come your bamalams, Red. I thought it was about time. Right now we ride for it."

A troop of Japanese cavalry came out from behind a Chinese warehouse about five hundred yards to the left rear. Another troop, on the gallop, appeared to the right, coming from near the Badakshan camp.

"Oi," the Yid said, as he kicked his horse in the ribs. "Dey vill cut it us off at de ford. I vish I had it vings."

"You'll have some in a few minutes," the Bean answered. "That is, if you've led a good life, Mr. Cohen. There's another troop. They flatter us sending three—"

"Three? You mean it a regiment. Look over dare to—oi, Red goes it down!"

JAPANESE INFANTRY CAME from a dry river bed and opened fire. Red's horse was hit and went down. So did Mr. Dolan, after sailing through the air. He lit on his head and if he had any less thick skull, he would not have been able to get up. As it was, he got up but stood, swaying back and forth.

The Yid and the Bean, as one man, turned their horses and rode for him. Jimmie Cordie beat them to Red, "Go on," he shouted. "Go on! I'll get him! Yid! Bean! Ride, you damn fools! I will—"

The Fighting Yid and the Boston Bean did not hear Jimmie. Or if they did, they paid no attention. When they reached Red, Jimmie was trying to get Red up behind him. Red was dazed and could not help at all. He weighed, as said before, some two hundred and thirty pounds and Jimmie, what with trying to hold in a plunging horse, could not handle him.

"Hold it my horse, Codfish," the Yid ordered, tossing the reins to the Bean, "I vill help Jimmie."

It was full time someone helped Jimmie Cordie. The Jap cavalry was getting close and the infantry seemed to be getting the range. The Yid, who was as strong as two average men, lifted Red up and Jimmie Cordie pulled. Together they got Red up on Jimmie's horse, behind Jimmie.

"Hang on, Red," Jimmie said, "Red! Snap out of it! Hang on to me."

Red had just about enough sense left to obey the order. He put one arm around Jimmie Cordie and took hold of the back of the saddle with a hand. The Yid remounted and they rode to where Carewe and Grigsby, instead of riding on, were waiting for them.

"We'll try the river," Jimmie said, calmly. "It's our only chance. *Allons, mes enfants!*"

It looked to be a more than slim chance. The river was wide and the current very fast. But it was, as Jimmie said, their only chance. The Japs had them cut off from every other avenue of escape.

The irrepressible Yid, with Jap bullets singing the death song all around, yelled to the Bean, "Hi, Beany! Ten smackers say dot I am a better svimmer dan you."

The Boston Bean grinned but did not answer. He was riding as close as he could to George Grigsby. The Bean did not like the way Grigsby was bent over in the saddle. It looked as if Grigsby might any moment fall out of it.

They made it to the river and without a second's hesitation, jumped their horses off the steep bank into the ice cold, rushing water. They were all hardbitted men in whose hearts was no fear. And they needed to be in jumping a horse into the river Tien-Tasi.

JIMMIE CORDIE CAME to the surface on his horse, Red still hanging on like grim death. But the horse only stayed up a moment. It had been too much weight for him to carry. Down he went and Jimmie and Red began swimming. The cold water had revived Red quite a little and he was able to swim with the current. The Yid, the Bean, and Carewe all came up on their horses. Grigsby's horse came up without Grigsby.

"George is under!" Carewe shouted. "He is—"

"I see him," the Bean answered, slipping off his horse.

Grigsby's head and shoulders had come up for an instant, then gone down.

"Und so do I see it him," the Fighting Yid announced, going off his horse like a polar bear goes off a rock into the water.

They both got hold of Grigsby under water and both came up with him. Grigsby was completely out, which was just as well. He was a big man and if he had struggled, the Yid and the Bean would have had a hard time with him. Grigsby was a swimmer himself and almost always calm and collected. But he had been wounded and there is no telling what he might have done.

"I got him," the Yid said. "Let go, Beany. I got it him."

"You have like heck. I'll keep his head up. Put his arm over my shoulder. His arm, you nitwit, not his leg," the Bean added after he came up. The Yid, in trying to do as ordered, had put the Bean under.

"Could I help it if his—oi!" Under went the Yid for a moment. But, under or not, they hung on to George Grigsby. Carewe's horse gave up and Carewe became as the rest, swimming for his life.

The Japanese lined the bank and shot at them as long as they were within sight, which was not very long.

The river widened out a mile or so below where the soldiers of fortune entered it and they made it to the opposite shore.

"Vell," said the Yid cheerfully, "here ve are," as he and the Bean carried Grigsby up the bank. "Vare do ve go from here, if de Captain please?"

"Anywhere you darn see fit," Jimmie answered, as he sat

down. "The captain stays right here until the captain gets his wind. Holy cats, that water was cold."

"It was so, Jimmie. Wan thing, though, it cleared the head ave me. How come us in the river? Last I remember was sailin' over the head ave me horse."

"We thought you needed a bath, Mr. Dolan," the Bean answered. "And, having plenty of time, decided to—George is coming to."

Jimmie Cordie got up and went over to where Grigsby was trying to sit up.

"Easy does it, George. Take your time. Anyone got anything on their hip?"

"I got a little brandy," the Yid said.

"Open it up."

A few minutes later, Grigsby got to his feet. "I'm all right, Jimmie."

"Let's go, then."

"Where?" demanded Red. " 'Tis on foot we are and all wet wid nawthin to—"

"At last, Mr. Cohen, Mr. Dolan admits he is all wet. You heard him admit it, didn't you?"

"I did, Codfisher; from now on, ve vill not even speak it to him as ve pass by."

"You will pass on High darn quick if we don't move out of here pronto," Jimmie Cordie said, with a grin, "Misto Jap will be across looking for us any minute."

"Where will we go, Jimmie darlin'? These two scuts I pay no attention to at all."

"Back in the country a little ways and then up stream. Right now back in the country and hole up. At night, up stream. That's all I can think of for the present."

"Can we build a fire and dry the clothes ave us?"

"We cannot. Get mad at the Yid and the Bean. The heat will dry your clothes, Terrance Aloysius. Can you make 'er, George?"

"Yes."

"If ye can't, 'tis me that will pack ye, George darlin'."

"Thanks, Red. I reckon I can stick around for a little while."

As they started for a thickly wooded track of timber, Red began an oration concerning the ancestry of the Bean and the Yid, to which they both listened very politely—until he ran out of breath.

"**I DO NOT** know," Major Shiga said, despondently. "We planned and it looked as if the Gods were smiling upon us. And now—Lieutenant-General Nagayo lies in his grave, our plans have all failed and—and—what is it all about, Colonel? I mean this killing of men and—"

Colonel Takara, riding beside Major Shiga, a little behind the ranking officers of a cavalry regiment, laughed, "You—one of the Samurai—ask that?"

"I know. But, ever since I looked upon the face of Lieutenant-General Nagayo, I have been thinking. It may be that after all there are other things besides war."

"You are downhearted, that is all. It is true our plans failed, but plans have failed since men were on the earth. We did not kill Lieutenant-General Nagayo. We killed what we thought was a worthless American mongrel."

"I wonder what happened to him?"

"Did I not tell you? His body was found in the rear of a house, a mile away from the place he was to have killed

Henry Pu-Yi. There were three bullets in it that had passed through his heart."

Major Shiga rode for a few moments, then said, "They are all dead shots, aren't they?"

"Yes, Major. Especially Captain Cordie. But soon we will see if they can withstand torture as well as they can shoot. They cannot escape us now."

"I do not know. You said that before—that our plan could not fail, and yet—I remember the squadron and the look on Lieutenant-General Nagayo's face as his life ebbed away because of our—"

"You must forget it," Takara commanded, curtly. "It is vital, Major. If it ever became known that you and I had anything to do with it, our careers would be ruined."

"That is so, Colonel. I will put it away from me. You say the Big Swords dogs cannot escape us this time?"

"Yes. I say it and I am sure of it. One of our planes picked them up yesterday. They have been joined by some two hundred odd men. The flyer said they looked to be Chinese. Evidently some of the T'aip'ing who helped Captain Cordie. If he—see, he is not so clever after all. If it had not been for the T'aip'ing, he could not have spoiled things for us. We have blocked them off from the west, the east and the south. There is only one way they can go and that is to the north. Now we ride to close that way from them."

Major Shiga looked back at the long files of troopers. "A regiment," he said, "a full regiment here and other regiments near. To take six soldiers of fortune and a few Chinese. I had rather that I met them with just as many men as they have. It would seem more in—"

"The regiments are not needed in the actual taking," Takara answered impatiently. "They were needed to properly cover the country, Major. It is like one of the hunts in the days of old.

"The game must be driven to the center and that takes many men." He was getting rather fed up with, as he termed Major Shiga, "this visionary young fool."

"I hope they will fight. I want to kill the one called the Bean and also Captain Cordie who mocked me. If there is a charge, I will lead it."

"You mean you will if given permission. There are many officers here who rank you, Major. Remember you are of the Intelligence and they are of the Line in command of their regiments. In a matter of the Intelligence you could call upon them for help but now it is simply a matter of exterminating a few Big Swords."

"I have already been given permission," Major Shiga answered, curtly.

"That is different, Major. I will charge at your side when we—here comes one of the advance guard. It may be that the game is flushed."

It was. The advance guard officer reported that the Big Swords officers with the Chinese had dug themselves in on top of a little knoll in a valley. The scouts ahead of the advance guard had run on to them as they entered the valley. The scouts, all but one, had promptly been shot down.

"We will not wait for the other units to close up," the Japanese Colonel in command of the regiment said. "We will—there goes the Twelfth regiment through the pass! They probably know what we know. Forward! The honor must be ours. No parley with the dogs. We will ride them down."

AS THE CAVALRY regiment got to the mouth of the valley, another regiment arrived, evidently with the same idea, that of riding down the Big Swords officers and the Chinese who could be plainly seen standing up behind the dirt thrown up from a hastily constructed star shaped trench. The two regiments started a race towards the knoll and just as they did, a third regiment came down the valley from the north end. Three thousand odd Japanese cavalrymen rode to gain much honor for themselves. Just where the honor came in riding over a few men, only they knew.

"I bet it my money on de bob-tail nag. Who bet it on de bay?" sang the Yid. "My, look at dem come. Anyvon would think ve wos made it of diamonds de vay dey—"

Rapid fire and machine guns opened up on the Japanese from the hills and the timber on both sides of the valley. Big Swords regiments of cavalry appeared where the Japanese regiments had entered the valley. The firing ceased and the Big Swords charged. The Japanese, thrown in momentary confusion, rallied, turned and met the Big Swords charge by a counter-charge of great fury.

"Holy mackinaw!" shouted Red Dolan. "The Big Swords have the little bamalam midgets! 'Tis a—Jimmie Cordie, did ye know they was there?"

"I did not. I hoped that they might be, Terrance Aloysius. But it did not look much like it a minute ago."

"How did ye—"

"For Pete's sake! I want to watch it, you redheaded ape. Listen, I sent some of the T'aip'ing to Chang right after the doings at the Altar. I knew darn well the Japs would chase us, so I asked for a Big Swords column to meet us around here. They have, Mr. Dolan. Now for heaven's sake, shut up."

"I will. Look at—"

"Oi, vot a ambush! Too bad dot de—"

"An ambush, Mr. Cohen," corrected the Bean. "An ambush, not a ambush. Your language is very painful for me to hear."

"Vot de hell difference does it make? It is a ambush just de same. My, see dem fight. De bamalam midgets are dare, ain't dey, Jimmie? I vish I vos down dare. Now de Japs learn it vot a real ambush is."

"Go ahead down. You'd—look coming. His horse is running away, I guess."

"No, it isn't, Jeems," the Boston Bean said. "Look at him jabbing the spurs in."

"It's a one man charge, Jimmie," Grigsby added. "Some Jap officer has gone loco."

"Looks that way. Don't hurt him if he makes it up here. By gosh, it's Major Shiga. He's coming to get you, Codfish."

"Get it behind Poppa," the Yid said. "Poppa vill not let de bad little bamalam hurt it you."

"Yeah?" The Bean stepped two or three paces away from the rest, his .45 held down by his side. "Here is where a bad little bamalam becomes a good one."

Major Shiga rode up and jumped off his horse. He ignored everything else but Jimmie Cordie. His gun was in its holster at his belt. Walking up to Jimmie and not halting until he was within three feet, Major Shiga said, "I have come for you, Captain Cordie."

"For me? You mean the Boston Bean, do you not?"

"No. I mean you. I am going to kill you, knowing that the next instant I will die myself. I will avenge the death of—"

"Wait a minute, Major. You are overexcited. I have my gun in my hand and yours is still in the holster. You are more apt to die the instant before than you are the instant after. Calm down and let's argue this thing out."

"No. I die for the honor of Nippon. My name will go down as the one who removed from the earth Captain Cordie of the Big Swords who flouted and tricked—"

"I'm afraid it won't, Major. It will go down as one who acted like a fool. Do you think you can draw and fire before I can pull trigger?"

"I know that I cannot. You are an officer. I challenge you to fight a duel. Service revolvers at ten paces, advance firing."

"I see. That is different. I accept your challenge, Major. And I will say this. If you kill me you may mount your horse and ride away. You gentlemen hear me? If Major Shiga kills me he is to mount his horse and ride away in full safety."

"We hear you, Jimmie," Grigsby answered, quietly.

BELOW IN THE valley a battle was raging, a battle to the death. Neither the Big Swords nor the Japanese asked for or gave quarter. Up on the knoll it was quiet, as the Japanese officer, ten paces away, faced the American soldier of fortune, in another battle to the death. Their revolvers were held, muzzles up as high as their heads, Major Shiga using his left hand.

Both of their faces were impassive as they waited Grigsby's word of command. Jimmie Cordie's eyes were impassive also. Major Shiga's eyes gleamed with a fanatical light.

Grigsby said, "Ready, gentlemen. One—two—three. Fire!"

Jimmie Cordie and Major Shiga dropped their gun muzzles and both walked forward. Bang—bang—bang—bang—bang—bang—Major Shiga spun around like a top, fell, raised himself to his knees, fired at Jimmie Cordie, who was falling, tried to get on his feet but could not make it. Jimmie Cordie fell face to the ground, rolled over, slowly got up on his feet, took two steps towards Shiga, who fired once more. Jimmie Cordie went back but as he did, put a bullet just above Shiga's heart.

"He's killed Jimmie," Red said, evenly. "That—little scut has killed Jimmie Cordie."

"He—has—like—heck. Carry me over to him—Red."

"Jimmie! Ye are not dead! Praise be—"

"Do as Jimmie says," Grigsby interrupted. "No talk, Red."

Major Shiga opened his eyes as Red knelt beside him, holding Jimmie Cordie in his arms.

"You—maintained the—honor of Nippon," Jimmie said, thickly through lips that seeped blood, "I—am—sorry— that you—that you—"

"I also am sorry," Major Shiga said, clearly. "It—we die, Captain Cordie. It may be that—that—war and—and— and—war is not the—best—" He died.

"Jimmie, are ye all right? Jimmie, answer me. Ye are scarin' the—George, is Jimmie dead?"

"No. His heart still beats. Put him down, Red."

"I will not, I will hold him in the arms ave me."

"You damn fool, do you want to make him die? He is

all doubled up. Put him down on the ground. Be careful with him."

Two Big Swords officers rode up, "Where is Captain Cordie?"

"There on the ground."

"Dead?"

"No. Badly wounded."

"The Lord Chang-lung Liang's compliments. The little men of Nippon, those in the valley, are destroyed but more come. We draw back in the hills."

"GEORGE! RED! JIMMIE has opened his eyes and is right sane! Oh, I'm so glad! Come in and see him!" Betty Ann turned and ran back into the hospital tent at Big Swords headquarters.

"I didn't get it an invite but I am goink too," the Yid announced.

"Me also," the Bean stated firmly.

"I also—not me also. My, but your language gives it me a pain in de ear."

"Score one on the shovel for you," the Bean said as they made for the tent.

Jimmie Cordie, two pillows under his head, grinned cheerfully as the four soldiers of fortune tiptoed up to the bed.

"Something tells me I've had quite a nap."

"A nap, is it? Ye have been goofy for a month, ye scut ave the world. What do ye mean by it, ye—it is not cryin' I am, it is the dust in me eyes. Jimmie—ye are well?"

"Yeah boy. I'm just foolin' around here because Betty Ann is my nurse. I guess I darn near hit the one way trail."

"You did, Jimmie. He got you four times."

"Yeah? Did I get him?"

"You did, Jeems, me good man. But you took a long time doing it. Why didn't you get him with the first shot. Very rotten shooting, I calls it."

"What? Ye stand there and tell Jimmie Cordie that—"

"That will do, Red. Go outside if you want to sound off."

" 'Tis right ye are, George. Pay no attention to the long legged scut, Jimmie darlin'."

"I won't, Red. Where is Carewe?"

"Over wid Chang. Old Mangali Boga is there too. The old scut could barely walk out ave the treasure house, wan of the Manchu chiefs do be tellin' me.

"He's hangin' around to see how ye are. Sahet Khan sent him word that if he had allowed you to get killed it would be just too bad for all Badakshans the Uryankhes met up wid."

"Well, Misto Jap will have to frame something else to get Uncle in a fight. Betty Ann, after you get all through nursing me, what are you going to do, go back to Kaintuck?"

"No, Jimmie. I am going to stay right here with my men folks and be nurse and everything. That darlin' old Chang says that I can have charge of the hospital. I shall become head of the nurses there."

"Oi, vill I get it vounded right avay! My, I am feelink sick right now. Move over, Jimmie, und let it a sick man lay down mit."

They all laughed at that and then Betty Ann ordered, sternly, "Go right out of here, all of you. My gracious goodness, reckon Jimmie must have some rest."

In San-sing, Colonel Takara, who had been slightly wounded in the head during the battle in the valley, sat at his desk. He was staring at the wall. "I will ask," he said slowly, aloud, "that I be detailed to one thing only and that is—to get Captain Cordie. I shall devote my life to doing that."

THY SON GROWS COLD

*Jimmie Cordie, ex–Foreign Legion Sergeant
and Adventurer-at-Large, uses an ominous
Chinese phrase to great advantage*

1

THE MANCHU PRINCESS Chi Huan laughed gaily as her cousin Kwang-si, who was walking beside her horse finished a story with "—and so Kauchau made the bows of ceremony and backed out of the audience chamber, his face as red as the silk on your sleeve."

The grim old leader of swords, commanding Chi Huan's escort, smiled as he heard the laughter. "Our golden one is happy," he said to the officer next to him, "Truly, youth is the time for— Out Swords! Yuan! Fan Chi! A circle three deep!"

From a pass that entered the valley through which Chi Huan and her escort were passing there had come a sudden rush of horsemen. Big men on stocky, long haired ponies. They rode yelling with glee, their swords flashing in the sunlight.

The Manchu princess had been on a visit to the city of Kitai and now was on her way home to Meng Wu, a walled city held by her father, Prince Chieh, in the foothills of the Thian Shan range, Sinkiang province, China. He had sent three hundred Manchu swordsmen to escort his daughter home.

In the hills, guns are scarce and ammunition even scarcer. Men there still fight with the sword as their ancestors fought for thousands of years before guns and gunpow-

der were invented. Prince Chieh could have sent a rifle
regiment and a battery to escort his daughter if he had
thought necessary. But it was only forty miles and the hills
were quiet; as quiet as they ever are, as far as he knew. So
he thought that three hundred Manchu swords would be
more than ample. Under ordinary conditions they would
have been, as all Chinese and most of the hill tribes avoid
Manchu swordplay as they would a king cobra.

What Prince Chieh did not know was that a strong
party of Uryankhes Tartars, who fear no swords, Manchu
or otherwise, were in the hills, high up so as to avoid curious eyes, with one objective, the taking of the Princess
Chi Huan. If any Chinese hunter or hillman were unlucky
enough to get close enough to the Tartars to see them, he
died right there. Prince Chieh's out patrols were far below

in the foothills. The Tartars waited until it was reported to the foray leader that the Princess Chi Huan had left Kitai, and then swooped down like a hawk on the prey.

The riders came on, riding as if to a festival, with shouts of laughter and songs of joy. And as they did, the Manchu sword circle was formed around the Princess Chi Huan.

Wang Hoi, leader of swords, walked over to where Chi Huan sat her horse. When the Tartars appeared she had drawn a Turkish scimitar from a golden sheath that hung from her silver and jade belt on linked chains of silver. For all her dainty, flowerlike beauty, Chi Huan was fighting Manchu to the marrow of her bones.

"Dismount, Princess of the Sinkiang Clans," Wang Hoi ordered calmly, "Our swords will lessen these hill jackals."

Chi Huan, aged fifteen, hereditary princess of the Sinki-

ang and princess of the House of Nurhachu, answered hotly. "What? I? Dismount? I will lead the charge that will send these pariah curs howling into the outer coldness."

"They are mounted, golden one in whose body there flames high the spirit of the Chieftain Nurhachu," Wang Hoi explained patiently, as if there were no such thing as charging Uryankhes within two hundred yards. "See, lotus bud, they outnumber us five to one. If we formed a wedge and charged, they would—"

"You are right, Wang Hoi. I dismount—but I will fight in the first ring of the circle."

WANG HOI WAS already on his way to where it looked as if a bunch of the Tartars would hit the first ring all at the same time and did not hear what Chi Huan said. Or, if he did, he had no time to argue with her.

The Manchu swordsmen, mostly young men, stood in their sleeveless silk fighting shirts, having discarded their outer robes. Their lithe young bodies were relaxed, swords resting easily across the left forearm. Those in the first ring stood far enough apart to allow free swordplay. The second ring stood about four feet back of the first, the third the same distance back of the second.

As the Tartar riders reached the circle, the Manchus did not give back an inch. There was a quick step to either side to avoid the plunging horse and then, the lightning fast upward and inward slash of Manchu sword.

In less than five minutes there was a hedge of dead and dying men and horses around the circle and in the hedge was the first ring of swordsmen.

Chi Huan saw her cousin, Kwang-si, who was two years older than she and very much like her in disposition, slip into the second ring that now became the first. She started right after him to get in herself. Chi Huan firmly believed that she was as good a swordsman as any of them, although at times she would admit that her handicap was a wrist not quite as strong as it might be.

An officer stepped in front of her and bowed. "Give room, Lord Shao," she commanded haughtily, "I go to fight at the head of the Clans."

The officer bowed again. "The Lord Wang Hoi gave command that the rings be not opened to admit—"

"The Lord Wang Hoi? I am the Princess of the Sinkiang Clans and the Lord Wang Hoi takes orders from me! I order that room be made for me instantly!"

"I cannot disobey an order given on the field of battle, oh resplendent Princess of the Sinkiang," answered Shao formally. "And yet you, the hereditary princess of the Sinkiang, give an order, also. Deign to pass your sword through my heart that I may ascend on High and have the Chieftains who sit and watch, pass on the matter for me."

"I withdraw the order," Chi Huan said hastily. She had known and liked the Lord Shao all her life. "I did not realize what I— See, Shao! The mongrels are forming a wedge!"

ERTOGHRUL, LEADER OF forays for Sahet Khan of the Uryankhes, led the wedge. It hit with a force that could not be withstood by any two-man circle in the world. The wedge went over the dead and dying and over the Manchu swordsmen.

Wang Hoi, master swordsman, died after making the wedge point less sharp and so did Lord Shao, trying to reach Ertoghrul, who had struck at and then evaded Wang Hoi.

Chi Huan ran to get into the fight, absolutely unafraid. She was of the blood that led the Manchus to the Peacock Throne of China and girl or no girl, she was going in. As she charged she looked like some gorgeous little butterfly in her gaily colored silks and sparkling jewels.

A Tartar leaned down from the saddle, arm outstretched to seize her, ignoring her sword. He kept right on going down after Chi Huan swayed to the left. Her sword had bitten deep into his shoulder.

The next rider reached for her also, only to get his forearm slashed from wrist to elbow. Then a horse bumped Chi Huan against another horse and a third Tartar got her, sword and all. She was about five feet, three inches tall and did not weigh over one hundred and ten pounds. In the grasp of the big Tartar, Chi Huan was a baby. He slapped the sword from her hand and then tucked her under his left arm, her face to his evil smelling sheepskin coat.

"Ho, brothers, I have her! Out! Out! To the hills, to the hills! I have her! Make way! I have the little one! Out! Out!"

The Tartars nearest to him took up the shout, "Out! Out! We have the little one! Cut! Slash! Slay! To the hills, brothers!"

There was a mad swirl of fighting, the Manchus still on their feet trying to reach the Princess Chi Huan. But they were hopelessly outnumbered. There was a final flurry, the Manchus putting every ounce of strength and all their swordplay into the effort, and then the Tartars rode for the hills with the Princess Chi Huan. Not very many of them after meeting three hundred Manchu swordsmen. Those that did ride, rode with triumphant shouts. They neither thought or cared about their dead and dying. To live, to feast, to fight, to die on the field of battle—what more could any man desire? So they rode, the wounded that could sit a horse singing as they swayed in the saddle.

Not a Manchu was on his feet when the Tartars disappeared into the pass. It was some minutes before there began a heaving and twisting among the piles of dead and wounded. Among a few that staggered to their feet or cleared themselves enough to sit up, was Kwang-si, Chi Huan's cousin. He had been more than lucky considering his size and fighting experience. Kwang-si had killed the first Tartar he encountered, wounded the second and had been parrying a cut from a third when another Tartar slashed at his head. An older Manchu parried the blow as best he could from where he was but the flat of his sword was beaten down on Kwang-si's head. The Manchu was not in position to throw the Tartar sword out and away from Kwang-si.

The boy went down as if hit by a giant hammer, out before his body reached the ground. When he came back to life there was a dead Tartar across his legs and a dead Manchu across his head and chest. The Manchu's body probably saved Kwang-si from getting his head kicked in by hoofs.

HE GOT UP and stood erect, swaying back and forth, blinking his eyes and shaking his head to clear his brain. All at once he realized that the Princess Chi Huan was not there and that there were only dead and wounded Manchus and Tartars in sight. Another young Manchu first sat up and then got on his feet, holding his head in both hands. This one had fared about the same as Kwang-si, only instead of being brought down by a sword he had been swept off his feet as the wedge broke the circle. When he had started to get up, something had hit him a glancing blow on the head and he had gone down again, out the same as Kwang-si. His head was bleeding but, again like Kwang-si, he was back in the land of the living.

A fatally wounded Manchu officer raised himself up on an elbow, blood trickling from his gray lips. In spite of it, he spoke distinctly: "The Princess Chi Huan of the Sinki-ang Clans is in the foul hands of the Uryankhes Tartars who live at the Lower Mountain. Do—nobles—of—the House of Nurhachu—stand still—instead of taking their princess—from—from—?" He fell back, dead.

"Get a sword, K'ung," ordered Kwang-si, kneeling to pick one up for himself. He dare not trust his aching head and stoop. "We will take the Princess Chi Huan from the Tartar jackals."

"Everything is going around and around," answered K'ung, a classmate of Kwang-si in the school of swords. "Get one for me, Kwang-si, and then bandage my head. You will have to lead me until the world stops spinning."

2

JIMMIE CORDIE, EX Foreign Legion sergeant and captain of machine gun company, A.E.F., one of the most famous soldiers of fortune in the Orient, lay stretched out on a rock ledge in the Thian Shan. He was watching through field glasses a column of riders two thousand feet below.

"Tartars," he announced. "It's too far south for the Altai Mountain Tartars. They may be—"

"Dey is Uryankhes Tartars," interrupted the man beside him. "I know it dem vell, Jimmie. Vonce dey chased de Boston Bean und me to de Afghan border. Ve made it mit de tail of de shirt und nothingk else. Oi, vot ve didn't lose on de vay is nobody's business. Bearers, Brownings, de jewels ve had got und de vorks, no foolin'. Dey is bad guys to fool mit, dem Uryankhes Tartars."

Jimmie Cordie laughed as he cased his glasses. "They must be if they can run you and the Codfish Duke ragged. Let's get back, Yid."

The Fighting Yid put his glasses up and followed Jimmie Cordie, who had started to crawl along the ledge. The Yid's right name was Abraham Cohen, born on Hester Street, New York City. But in the A.E.F., where he had been a first sergeant of a machine gun company, he was renamed the Fighting Yid. Later in the Orient, he remained the

Fighting Yid. And he was one. He would fight anything at any time, regardless of odds.

"I vish dot ve could have taken it a couple of shots at dem," he said, as a wider place enabled him to crawl up beside Jimmie Cordie.

"Yeah? You may get the chance yet, Mr. Cohen. Stick around and hope for the best. If they spot us up here, you'll get all the— Well, for Pete's sake! Look at Red up on his feet."

The ledge ended at a fairly level space about twenty feet wide on the side of which was a spring. Two men were sitting near the spring and a third man standing up.

"Didn't I tell you to keep off that leg, you big red-headed ape?" demanded Jimmie, as he and the Yid arrived.

"Ye did, Jimmie darlin'," Red Dolan, ex Foreign Legion and lieutenant of military police A.E.F. answered. " 'Tis me that will admit it. I was just tryin' to see if it would hold me up at all." The big, two hundred and thirty odd-pound Irishman grinned triumphantly.

"Well, now that you have seen that it will, sit down again."

"Und do it mit de vell known snap, Irish bummer, or me und Jimmie vill kick from you de slats," the Yid added.

"Oh, ye will?" demanded Red. "Ten Hester Street scuts and twenty-wan more added to them and—"

"Let's dispense with that chatter for a few minutes," one of the seated men interrupted. "Or take the Yid out somewhere, Red, and tell him about the number of Yids and Cordies it will take."

"Both of you put a jaw tackle on," commanded Jimmie

Cordie. "They were Uryankhes Tartars, according to the Yid, George."

"Not so good," answered George Grigsby, ex Foreign Legion and major of infantry A.E.F. and since the war, fighter in the far places. "If the Uryankhes are up we better stay right here until Red and the Bean are able to travel. Their wounds won't stand much fussing around for a week or so."

JIMMIE LOOKED AT the man sitting beside Grigsby. "How do you feel, Bean?" The Bean, who was listed in the Massachusetts Social Register as John Cabot Winthrop, grinned and raised his right arm about a foot and moved it a little. He was tall, lean and lanky, with a sorrowful looking face and eyes that hid a happy-go-lucky-nature and an absolutely reckless, devil-may-care heart. He had served in the Legion with Jimmie Cordie, Red Dolan and George Grigsby and in the A.E.F. as a captain of artillery. And he was called anything that even remotely suggested his birthplace, Boston.

"Well, Jeems, me good man, it is much better than it was yesterday. I can at least pull trigger."

"And that is about all, Codfish. Well, Here is the way she stacks up to me. We've got one Browning, our thirty-thirty rifles, our Colts, not much ammunition, no bearers and some iron rations. The Yid and I can't pack the Browning and do any fighting at the same time to help George out. I think we better hole up right here where there is good water and wait until Red and the Bean get well enough to do business at the old stand. We can last ten days on—"

"You know vot I vish?" asked the Yid. "I vish dot de Var

Lord of Shangtun vos in de northvest corner of de hot place mit a southvest gale blowingk."

"The black curse ave Cru'mel on the double crossing snake in the grass," Red started. "The monkey-faced cross between a pink eyed gibbon and a polecat! In we go to his city wid four hundred bearers and scrappin' Chinks that we spent many the weary day trainin'. In we go wid them and eight machine guns and—"

"Out we come with one machine gun and no bearers or scrappers," Jimmie Cordie finished for him, with a grin. "That's water long since under the bridge, Mr. Dolan. We had a perfect right to trust him. Personally I think we are blame lucky to have been able to remove ourselves from his midst with our hair still on, the way his noble army jumped us. Forget it and let's figure a way out of the hills. If there is—" There came a sound as if a pebble had been dislodged and was rolling down a rock. Before the sound died away, Jimmie Cordie, the Yid and Grigsby were on their feet, their .45 Colt revolvers in their hands. Red and the Boston Bean drew their guns from where they sat, the Bean with his left hand. It was the instant, automatic reaction of veterans to threatened danger.

There was a split second's pause, then they heard a voice, "No shootie! No shootie! Fliends! No shootie, honolable Captain!"

Jimmie Cordie laughed and holstered his Colt. "I know that voice. Advance, friends."

DOWN FROM THE top of a nearby boulder slid Kwang-si and K'ung. They both walked up to Jimmie Cordie, halted, then bowed. "Hullo, Kwang-si. Hullo, K'ung. What the dickens are you doing way up here in the hills?"

"We go to lescue the Plincess Chi Huan," answered Kwang-si in English, of which he was very proud. "Now that we have found you, our honolable elder blothels, can do light away."

There is no 'r' in the Chinese language, which is now spoken by Manchus. Few Manchus or Chinese can make a sound like it. If the letter ends a word it can be managed but at the beginning or surrounded by other letters, very seldom. An' 'l' is substituted.

Prince Chieh had at one time been first secretary of the Chinese Embassy, Washington and his daughter Chi Huan had gone to school in Chevy Chase, a suburb. On her return to Meng Wu she had established a school of English, with herself as teacher, for her favorites, Kwang-si and K'ung had both attended the school and both could speak and understand English very well, save for the fatal "r."

"Go do what?" yelled Red. "Rescue Herself? From who? Ye stand there bowin' and grinnin' and Herself to be rescued, ye half pints ave nothin' at all?"

"Calm down, Mr. Dolan," Jimmie said. "Let's get at it. Start from the beginning, Kwang-si."

The soldiers of fortune had twice fought for Prince Chieh during the time he was forced to defend his territory from ambitious generals who sought to control the North. They all knew and loved the little Manchu princess. And she, in turn, called them her "honolable blothels."

Red had completely won her heart by showing her how to operate a machine gun and letting her fire several rounds. To Red, Chi Huan was "Herself" and woe betide anyone who crossed her.

"We go to rescue the Princess Chi Huan from the Uryankhes Tartars, honorable elder brothers. The Uryankhes of the Lower Mountain."

"How did they take the Princess Chi Huan?" Grigsby asked.

KWANG-SI TOLD OF the fight, ending with, "So we found our swords and started after the Princess Chi Huan. We saw the Tartars cross a pass and we climbed to avoid them. We knew that we could not rescue the Princess by force."

"Well," the Boston Bean said gravely, "considering the fact that there are some five thousand Uryankhes and you have only two swords, I think your decision a wise one."

Kwang-si grinned. "We know where their encampment is and now that we have found you, we will go there and lesson the Tartar mongrels, get the Princess and go home." Any idea that the five men he had seen repulse charge after charge of veteran infantry at Meng Wu would have any trouble in lessoning five thousand Uryankhes, did not enter his mind.

"We'll go and do that little thing," Jimmie answered. "Before we start, though, what else do you know about the Uryankhes, Kwang-si?"

"Pleny else, honorable Captain. Very bad tribe, indeed. Robbers—murderers—thieves and all that is bad. Very brave though," he added with Manchu fairness. "They will stand up to our swords. In the lessoning may I shoot the little gun that goes lat-tat-lat tat?"

K'ung was not nearly as good at English as Kwang-si but he was good enough to know that it seemed as if Kwang-si was beating him to the machine gun provided the honorable elder brothers would let anyone shoot it but themselves.

He promptly announced, "I am a very, very good shot, honorable Captain. May I shoot the little gun that goes lat-tat?"

Jimmie laughed. "If the chance comes you may shoot it. How far is it to the Lower Mountain, Kwang-si?"

"From here—" Kwang-si stopped to figure. "From here to River Talim, twenty miles as the birds fly. From there—thirty or forty. That is all—I do not know how to figure it in English."

"We'll figure it. Who is their Khan?"

"Sahet Khan," answered Kwang-si.

"Do you know anything about him?"

"Yes, resplendent Captain. Once my all powerful father, before he went on High, went to the Tartar encampment and I went with him. My mighty father was fliendly with Sahet Khan. But even so he took with him five regiments. We stayed a month there and I played with Zagatai, who is Sahet Khan's favorite son. He is two years younger than me."

"How long ago was this, little brother?"

"Three years."

"You say that Zagatai is his favorite son?"

"Very much so. Zagatai does as he pleases and Sahet Khan only laughs. No one else even dares to look as if they wished to do what Zagatai does. He is Sahet Khan's sun and moon and all that is precious."

"Jimmie," protested Red, "what the hell are ye wastin' all this time for? Herself is in the hands av the wildmen and here ye sit wah-wahin' wid a couple av kids."

"Listen, Terrance Aloysius. The way we are hooked up we couldn't get within twenty miles of the encampment and if we did by some fluke, we couldn't penetrate fifty feet towards the center of it. The Uryankhes are not Chinese to be smacked out of the way. If we had what we started this little excursion with we couldn't do 'er. The only way to get Herself out of their hands is to frame 'em—and that is why I am asking questions. It may be that I can bring something out to hang the said frame on. You sabe, Mr. Dolan?"

"Right ye are, Jimmie darlin'. Well I know ye can do it, me bucko. Go ahead wid the questions."

KWANG-SI KNEW A lot about the encampment and the Uryankhes, providing things had not changed since his visit. Finally Jimmie said, "All right, Kwang-si. You and K'ung can go over and inspect Mr. Browning's masterpiece."

The two young Manchus made it to the gun in a dead heat. During the defense of Meng Wu, all of the school of swords had hung around as close as they could, to the machine gun section and not get driven away by the master of swords. It was war and they had no chance. But no one but her father had any authority over Chi Huan and she had shot Red's gun, much to her delight and the envy of the entire school of swords.

"Well," Jimmie said, "instead of being in need of a rescue party, we become one. One thing is dead open and shut and that is as long as we can't lick 'em, we got to frame 'em. The question before the house is—how?"

"Think up something," demanded Red, who had unlimited confidence in Jimmie Cordie.

"And hurry it up, Jeems," the Boston Bean added.

"Yeah? It may take me all of three minutes to think up something that will take the Princess Chi Huan away from the Uryankhes Tartars. Can you wait that long?"

"Sneak it up on dare blind side," suggested the Yid, as he settled back in a more comfortable position against a rock. "Und now dot I have told how to did it, poppa vill take it a nap vile de children figure."

"Sneak up on the blind side is good," Jimmie said. "If the Uryankhes have a blind side I never heard about—" Jimmie stopped and looked over at Kwang-si and K'ung.

Red opened his mouth to say something, caught Grigsby's eye and closed his mouth again.

At last Jimmie laughed. "It might work, at that. It's the only thing I know that's got the ghost of a chance."

"No doubt it will," the Bean agreed solemnly. "We all think it will now that you have explained it so clearly. There isn't a flaw in it."

"I just thought of an old American custom," Jimmie answered with a grin, then called Kwang-si over.

3

"HO, FATHER, ERTOGHRUL comes!" shouted the youngest and favorite son of Sahet Khan, as he rushed headlong into Sahet Khan's tent. "He brings with him a Chinese maiden who wears a sword sheath of gold and jewels. Say I may have it! Mine is worn and only of leather. Say that I may have it!"

"Silence," roared the old Khan who was sitting on a priceless rug looted from some caravan. Four or five women of various ages were reclining on smaller rugs near him. All were eating from plates filled with candied ginger and fruits. "Am I a dog to be interrupted by the bellowing of a calf not yet dry behind the ears, while I am eating? Or am I one who orders the Yak Tails carried before me as a true descendant of Genghis Khan? Out! You have not learned yet how to handle a sword, and yet you want a golden sheath."

One of the women laughed. The boy, not yet fourteen, turned on her like a young wildcat, his fierce dark eyes blazing with anger. "You laugh at me, fat pig. I will slit your throat with my knife." As he spoke he was drawing a dagger from his belt and before he got to "my knife" had hurled himself at the woman. She rolled swiftly away but would not have gained safety if Sahet Khan, with a quickness belied by his bulk and age, had not reached out and caught the boy by the leg. He drew Zagatai to him, disarmed him and held him close to a massive chest.

"Quiet," Sahet Khan soothed, as Zagatai struggled to get free. "Quiet, little son of mine. It is not well for a woman to laugh at a descendant of the Great Wolf, is it, Khan to be? Neither is it well to draw steel in the presence of your Khan, oh shameless one. Stop struggling and stand up. Then tell your news and voice your requests like a man."

Zagatai stopped kicking and squirming and Sahet Khan stood him on his feet, laughing as he did so. Kwang-si had told the truth when he said that Zagatai could do anything with Sahet Khan. Born of a young wife that the old Khan really loved, the boy could take more liberties with Sahet Khan than anyone else in the world.

"Ertoghrul comes, as I have said," Zagatai began, glaring at the woman who was cautiously making her way back to her rug. She was already planning to make some of Zagatai's favorite candy for him so there might be peace between them. "He brings with him a Chinese maiden as captive. She wears a golden sheath. May I have it?"

"If you desire it," answered Sahet Khan indifferently, "and can find a sword that fits it. To your tents, you women. Remain here with me, little son. Eat your fill of the candied fruits."

"I am not hungry, father. I have but just left the tent of my mother. She sent her love to you."

Sahet Khan laughed. "Ho! You finally remembered that, did you? Such all unimportant matter as the love of a woman is to be remembered and forgotten at will?"

Like all Tartars, Sahet Khan loved children and would play with them by the hour. No matter how merciless against a foe or how hard in dealing with men, any Tartar will stop and lift a child up to be cuddled against a weatherbeaten cheek. And, like the Afghans, the Tartars have a well developed sense of humor.

THE WOMEN LEFT the tent and a few minutes later, Ertoghrul entered with the Princess Chi Huan. The little Manchu was very angry and it was quite evident, did not care who knew it. She still looked like a gorgeous butterfly, even if her silken robes were more or less bedraggled. On the way to the Tartar encampment she had been put on a horse, she had eaten when they ate and slept when they slept, covered by a sheepskin coat tossed to her by Ertoghrul.

Now, as she stood in front of Sahet Khan, who was feared the length and breadth of the hills, her head was held high and her midnight black eyes were blazing with wrath.

"Here is the maiden you sent me for," Ertoghrul announced.

"So I see. Go to the horse lines and pick out any ten that please you."

"Thanks, Sahet Khan. I lost many riders taking her. The Manchus fought to the death."

Ertoghrul swaggered out of the tent and as he did, Zagatai pointed to Chi Huan's sword sheath. "See, Father? There it is. May I have it now?"

Chi Huan did not understand what he said but she saw the gesture and sensed that he had asked for the sheath. It was the last straw as far as she was concerned and she went into action, speaking Pushtu, the universal language of the border. "You dare? You dare, hill jackal? Put a sword in the sheath and then get one for yourself and see if you can take it!"

Zagatai's little brown hand flashed to his knife hilt and the flame that leaped into his eyes matched the one in Chi Huan's eyes. "You call me hill jackal, Chinese maiden? I will bury my knife in your heart." He understood and spoke Pushtu as did Sahet Khan.

"Ho! Ho!" bellowed the old Khan. "The maiden has defied you, oh descendant of the Great Wolf. Can you find her a sword and then fight her for the sheath?" he teased.

Zagatai's fierce, clean-cut little face became puzzled and his hand fell away from the dagger hilt. "But—but—I cannot fight a girl with swords," he answered, a little uncertainly.

"Then how are you going to get the sheath, oh Khan to be? Unless your father takes it for you and gives it to you. If you cannot figure a way to get it yourself will the riders follow you into battle after I am gone, knowing that you relied on me to get you what you desired?" The old Khan was thoroughly enjoying himself.

"How can I get it if I cannot— Will you give me the sheath, Chinese maiden? I will give you for it whatever—"

"I? Chinese? I am Manchu—hill jackal! If you call me Chinese but once more I will flesh my sword in your—" Chi Huan stopped, realizing she had no sword to do anything with.

SAHET KHAN SETTLED back on his rug, supporting himself by an elbow. It was as good as a puppet show to watch and listen to these children. He egged them on by asking blandly. "What do you say to that, oh peerless warrior who still lacks the sheath?"

Zagatai did not say anything for a moment, then he suddenly smiled. "I withdraw the Chinese, oh most beautiful Manchu maiden. And I am not a jackal. I am Zagatai, son of Sahet Khan, descendant of Genghis Khan, the Great Wolf."

Chi Huan, true Manchu, decided that her chances of escape might be enhanced if she were friendly with Zagatai, so she in turn smiled. "I withdraw the jackal, son of Sahet Khan, descendant of the Great Wolf whose fame still rings all over the world. You come from a line of heroes. See—I present you with the sheath and some day, if you come to my city of Meng Wu, I will fit a hero's sword into it for you."

Chi Huan, while she was talking, had unbuckled her belt and handed it out to Zagatai, sheath and all.

As Zagatai reached for it with eager hands, Sahet Khan laughed. "Now you have what you want because you made friends. When you cannot fight, make friends and get what you want that way. Take the maiden to your mother's tent, little son. She is under your protection. See to it that no harm comes to her."

"Why was I taken?" demanded Chi Huan haughtily. "Do you not know that my father will make of this place a waste in which even jackals cannot live?"

"I took you for a Chinese who will soon come for you, little one. Go now, with my son, to his mother's tent. She will take care of you. I wish to sleep." Sahet Khan's head went down on the cushions and after looking at him for a moment, Chi Huan followed Zagatai out of the tent.

"Do you know any tricks with a sword, Manchu maiden?" Zagatai asked, as they walked along. "If you do, will you teach them to me? I am learning fast but would like to know more. You offered to fight me, so you must know some."

"Certainly I know some," answered Chi Huan. "Many of them. If you tell me of this Chinese dog who is coming for me, it may be that I will show you how; to play them."

"I don't know anything about it," answered Zagatai, truthfully and regretfully. "If you will show me the tricks I will give you one of my ponies to ride."

"After I am rested, get two swords and I will show you," Chi Huan answered. She thought that with a pony and a sword she might escape. Which was a very optimistic thought considering that she was surrounded by five thousand odd Tartar swordsmen and riders.

4

THE TARTAR ENCAMPMENT held a great many captives who were treated as slaves. Chinese, Uzbegs, Persians, Kirghis and others taken in raids on caravans. They were working all over the place around the tents and the horse lines. So when a slender figure dressed in coolie robes got in Zagatai's way one morning, the son of Sahet Khan hardly looked up. "Out of the way, dog," he ordered, "When you see a— you, Kwang-si?"

Kwang-si put down the pail of water he was carrying and grinned. "Yes, it's me. Do not show surprise, Zagatai. Act natural."

Zagatai, who had been boon companions with Kwang-si during the latter's visit to the encampment, asked eagerly, "Are you playing a game, Kwang-si? Let me play also. What are you doing dressed in those clothes? Is your father here? Where are the regiments?"

"One question at a time. Yes, I am playing a game. It may be that you can also play. These clothes I took from one I met in the hills. My honorable father has ascended on High. I have no regiments. Take me somewhere we can talk without notice being taken."

"We will go to my mother's tent. There we—no, that is not the place to go, there is a Manchu maiden there."

"A maiden? I do not like them. They laugh and talk too

much and want to play silly games. Think of some other place if you want to play in the game with me. Some riders are already looking this way, surprised that you stand and talk so long to a slave. Loudly order me to follow you with the pail."

Zagatai dearly loved any kind of a game and had not, in any way, connected Kwang-si with the Princess Chi Huan. As a matter of fact, Zagatai did not know what a Manchu was, Chi Huan had insisted that she was one, so Zagatai had agreed that she was. To him she was Chinese, although her eyes did not slant up at the corners, as was Kwang-si. The eyes of the pure blooded Manchu do not slant up, but Zagatai did not know, or care anything about it. There were many Chinese at the encampment and he classed Chi Huan and Kwang-si as Chinese because he knew they spoke it.

"Follow me," he commanded loudly. "I do not care whose slave you are or where the water is going. Pick up the pail and follow me. Quickly or the whip will curl around your body."

He led the way over to a tent near the horse lines that he knew was empty. Once inside, he drew the flap across the entrance and said, "Now tell me? Have you seen my father? How did you get into the encampment past the outer patrols?"

KWANG-SI SMILED AS he sat down on a stool. As he did he felt around his waist as if moving something up a little.

"What have you got under your robe?" demanded Zagatai, former questions forgotten.

"Nothing," answered Kwang-si hastily. "I got here by the path you showed me when we were playing hill robbers.

Three times patrols passed me but each time I hid from them, I found the pail and—"

"I know you have something hidden around your waist," insisted Zagatai. "Show it to me, Kwang-si."

"If I do, will you promise not to ask for it?"

"Yes, I promise. What is it?"

Kwang-si lifted his robe and displayed a cartridge belt full of cartridges from which hung a holstered .45 Colt revolver.

Zagatai drew a long breath. He stood there, his eyes full of longing, his little fists clenched.

"I—I am sorry I promised," he said finally. "Let me see it."

"You do see it."

"I mean, take it in my hand. Take it off and let me wear it for a minute. Is the gun all right?"

"Yes," answered Kwang-si, taking off the belt and handing it to Zagatai. "If you take the gun out, be careful. It is loaded. A pull here and it shoots."

"I know guns," Zagatai answered, glaring at Kwang-si.

"Show me that you do, then. You may wear it while I am telling you about—"

"I will give you five ponies for it and—and—all that I have you may want."

"It is not to be traded for. Sit down and keep quiet. It may be that if you help me there will be a gun and belt just like that one, for you."

"I will help you," answered Zagatai promptly. "How do you take the bullets out?" He drew the Colt from the holster.

"I thought you knew guns? Give it to me and I will show you."

Zagatai handed the gun over, very reluctantly. "I do know most guns but not this one."

Kwang-si showed how to eject the cartridges and then reload. After Zagatai had the gun once more, Kwang-si began a story. It was a long one all about how he had run away from school, met three Englishmen in the hills and guided them through the passes to a temple they wished to see. Finally the Englishmen were attacked by a band of masterless men and the bearers were all slain. The Englishmen, with Kwang-si, retreated to a cave far up in the hills and there, according to Kwang-si, they died of their wounds. All they had left in the way of weapons were three guns and belts of cartridges. So Kwang-si buried the Englishmen by rolling their bodies to the brink of a precipice and pushing them over, hid two of the guns and belts, took one and started for the Uryankhes Tartars. He knew he could not make his own city, being alone. He saw the Lower Mountain and knew he was close to the Tartars. It was a story that could have been shot full of holes by an older, wiser person but Zagatai swallowed it, hook, line and sinker.

He had paid more attention to aiming the Colt at imaginary enemies than he had to the story.

"How far is it from here?" he demanded. "If I get the guns I can keep them as spoils of war. Otherwise my father or whoever went to get them would—"

"That is just the reason I sneaked into the encampment. I could have come in boldly and demanded the protection due my father's son. But I thought of you and I wanted you to have a gun and belt also. The other we can trade. Then you are to help me get to a walled city I know."

"You did exactly right," Zagatai said firmly, "and as I would have done. We will go and get the guns and—"

"I have planned this way," interrupted Kwang-si. "We can slip out tonight and get to the place before morning. One gun and belt is yours. The other we will trade, each taking half of what we get for it."

"That is a fine plan, Kwang-si. I know a way we can go and the patrols cannot see us at all. Will we need horses? If we do we cannot go the way I know because horses cannot climb the mountain side."

"No, we do not need horses. It is less than ten miles. Many times we have gone further than that and been back by noon."

"That is so. I will tell no one—not even my mother. You can wait in this tent, Kwang-si. I will bring food."

"All right, Come as soon as you can after dark. And do not forget the food, I am very hungry. You still have my gun and belt."

Zagatai unbuckled the belt and handed it over, very slowly. "I will wear mine home," he announced as he left the tent.

5

"HERE THEY COME," Jimmie Cordie said, looking over a clump of brush to the side of a steep mountain pass. "We'll let them get right up to the mouth of the cave, Yid. Look at the little Tartar swagger along."

It was just breaking dawn. Zagatai could not get away from his mother as soon as he thought he could.

"I'll do the dirty work at the crossroads," Jimmie went on. "You stay here, Kwang-si may not have put it over as completely as he looks. If anything happens, try to get Kwang-si in the clear."

"Vot could happen?" demanded the Yid. "Ve can see all over. Vare could it any-von come from?"

"The Uryankhes don't have to come from, Mr. Cohen. It is a sad case of all of a sudden they are here. Get set, Yid."

Kwang-si halted at the mouth of a cave, Zagatai beside him, "Here it is, just as I left it. The guns are in the cave under some—"

Both he and Zagatai whirled around as they heard a cold voice say, in Pushtu, behind them, "Put your hands up above your heads."

To Zagatai, for an instant, the white man standing there was one of the Englishmen come back to life. Then he saw a little smile on Kwang-si's lips and knew he had been tricked.

The little Tartar crouched, ignoring the gun in the white man's hand, drew his dagger and launched himself straight at the white man's throat.

Jimmie Cordie sidestepped and caught Zagatai in mid-air, his left arm going around Zagatai's waist. He did not want to hurt the little Tartar but he knew that until he got the knife, Zagatai was as dangerous as a leopard cub. So he upended Zagatai, hoping to shake the knife loose. Instead of doing that, Jimmie felt the knife being driven through his leather puttees and into his leg, then withdrawn for another thrust. So he did the only thing he could do; he rapped Zagatai sharply over the knife hand knuckles with the barrel of the Colt. Zagatai's hand opened and the knife fell to the ground. Jimmie swung him rightside up and set him on the ground, letting go of him as soon as Zagatai's feet got firm hold.

As soon as his feet touched the ground, Zagatai turned so that he could see Kwang-si. Ignoring Jimmie, he began telling Kwang-si just who and what he, Kwang-si, was from the viewpoint of a Uryankhes Tartar who had been trapped by a supposed friend.

KWANG-SI LISTENED WITH an air of polite, grave attention until Zagatai ran out of breath, then answered, "I regret that you feel as you do, oh descendant of the Great Wolf Genghis Khan. This—to explain matters to you. The Manchu Princess Chi Huan who is now a captive of the Uryankhes Tartars is a close blood relation of mine and is also the hereditary princess of the Sinkiang Clans of which my House of Kwang is one. Therefore, I was justified in using any means to free the Princess Chi Huan. This you will admit as a Tartar, also of pure blood."

"But—but—you should not have tempted me with the gun and belt," answered Zagatai hotly. "The rest is as you say. You were justified in playing a trick but to tell me that I could also have a gun and—"

"Wait a minute, son of Sahet Khan," Jimmie interrupted. "Did Kwang-si promise you a gun and belt?"

"Yes, white man. No—that is not true. He told me that he knew where there were two and said that I could have one of them."

"Listen, Zagatai. We have come for the Princess Chi Huan. Now that we have you, we will offer to exchange the descendant of the Great Wolf for the Manchu princess. No harm will come to you in the meanwhile if you behave yourself. Has any harm been done to the Princess Chi Huan?"

"No. She is an honored guest in the tent of my mother," answered Zagatai, not at all afraid.

"Then you also will be an honored guest with us until the exchange is made."

Zagatai laughed scornfully. "You cannot get out of the land with me, Englishman. My father and my brothers and the men of my mother's family and all the riders will comb the hills for me. And when my father takes you, you will sit on the sharpened stick until you die—all three of you. Until my father comes, do in as you please with me. I am not afraid of you." The Yid had come up while Zagatai was talking.

"We know that you are not afraid," Jimmie answered, "and as you say, we will do as we please. At the moment, it pleases me to do this." He had holstered his Colt and now he took off his cartridge belt and held it out to Zagatai, holstered Colt and all. "You were told of a gun and belt. Here is one for you."

Zagatai reached for the belt, then withdrew his hand. "There is another trick," he declared.

"No there isn't. Only this—in way of a warning. You see this man," pointing to the Yid. "He will be watching you all the time as will Kwang-si. If you attempt to draw and fire the gun without their permission, they will kill you. It is your gun and belt, forever, but you are not to shoot it until told that you can. Is that plain to you, oh Zagatai?"

"Yes, it is plain," Zagatai answered. "Give it to me."

"Let me take it a minute, old kidt," the Yid said. "I vill make it de belt shorter for you so dot it fits around de waist," then he remembered that Zagatai probably could not understand English and repeated in Pushtu. Zagatai looked at the Yid for a moment, then handed the belt over.

A little later Jimmie asked, "All ready?"

"Sure," answered the Yid cheerfully, "'ve make it in ten hours, I bet you."

"All right. I'll give you that much time and a little more before I go calling on Sahet Khan. Zagatai, take things easy and you'll land home with a gun and belt. Try to pull any Tartar tricks and there will be a new Tartar kid's face in the angel chorus. Translate that for him on the way, Kwang-si. Get going."

6

THE NEXT MORNING a Tartar patrol saw a man, who looked to be without weapons of any kind, calmly walk down one of the passes that led to the encampment. There were four riders in the patrol and as one man, they drew swords and put spurs to their ponies.

Jimmie Cordie, as they got near, halted and held up a white handkerchief. The riders pulled up about five feet away from him. There was no hurry and they might as well listen to what this white man had to say. They had all fought against the English and placed Jimmie as one.

"I go to see Sahet Khan," Jimmie announced in Pushtu.

"Oh, you do, Englishman?" the leader of the patrol snarled. "Well, what you will see and also feel, is the edge of my sword. Down on your knees and beg for your life. It may be that I will spare it and let you live as my slave."

"Speaking of your sword," Jimmie answered. "If I feel the edge of it there is no doubt but what you very shortly afterwards will feel the point of the sharpened stick entering your vitals. I go to tell Sahet Khan of his son, Zagatai. Now what, oh mighty leader of a small patrol?"

"How can you, an Englishman, have anything to tell the Khan of the Uryankhes about his son? You are—"

"As you delay me here the son of Sahet Khan—grows cold."

The Tartars knew what that meant. It was Chinese. Not Chinese language but a sinister Chinese warning. It warned of death to come to a beloved one, unless— The warning whir-r-r-r of a rattlesnake.

"Mount behind me," the Tartar leader said hastily. "We will take you to Sahet Khan."

THREE HOURS LATER, Jimmie Cordie, American soldier of fortune stood in front of Sahet Khan of the Uryankhes Tartars, in Sahet Khan's tent.

"I am Sahet Khan. Who are you?"

"I am James Cordie, an American who—"

"You start with a lie. You are an Englishman. I have fought too many of them not to know one when I see him."

"An American is from a land that was once owned by the English," Jimmie explained courteously. "And so the Americans are very much like them. I have come for the Manchu Princess Chi Huan."

"By the sacred Yak Tail banner of Genghis Khan! You are crazy, Englishman. I will order the fools that brought you to me, flayed—and you with them. You come for the Manchu maiden, do you? Where is your army, crazed one?"

"I haven't any," Jimmie answered with a grin. "Before I start telling you the sad story of why I haven't an army, it might interest you to know that—thy son, Zagatai, grows cold."

Sahet Khan tensed and his right hand flashed to his sword hilt. "Stand very still—very-very still—American," he commanded. "Say that again."

Jimmie Cordie knew that he was as close to death as he could be and not meet it, yet there was no change in his voice and the smile remained in his eyes and on his lips, as he repeated, "Thy son, Zagatai, grows cold."

Sahet Khan called out and a Tartar guard came in. "Go to the tent of the mother of my son, Zagatai, and see if he is there. If he is not—find him and bring him here to me."

As the tent flap dropped back into place behind the guard, Jimmie said, "He will not find your son, Sahet Khan. We have him. Give us the Princess Chi Huan and we will, in exchange, give you your son."

"We? Who is we? You dare to come to me, Sahet Khan, with a smile on your lips and tell that you have his son? What lie is this? You die slowly, fool."

"As I die—at the same time, so dies your son, Zagatai. Keen eyes watch from the hills, Sahet Khan."

"Are they close enough to see you being lowered into the boiling oil and close enough to have the ears that are near the eyes hear your screams for mercy?"

"They can see through their glasses but I doubt if the ears are close enough to hear my screams over the screams of your son, Zagatai."

Sahet Khan started to draw his sword, hesitated, shoved it back in the sheath and then—laughed.

"Ho! You are a man, American. I also am a man and know one when I look deep into his eyes. Sit down and tell me of this thing."

Jimmie Cordie sat down on a rug and Sahet Khan sat down on another.

"It is this," Jimmie said. "You captured the Princess Chi Huan. I have captured your son, Zagatai. According to Zagatai, the Princess has been treated as an honored guest. Therefore, your son receives the same treatment."

"In the taking, was my son hurt in any way?"

"No," answered Jimmie with a grin. "He did all the hurting that was done. Your son runs true to his blood, Sahet Khan. He crouched, drew his knife and sprang at my throat as if all the Uryankhes Tartars were backing him up. I caught him in the air and turned him upside down, not wanting to hurt him. As I did I got his knife in my leg." Jimmie turned his leg so that Sahet Khan could see a cut in the puttee. The Yid had given Jimmie rough first aid and bandaged the wound with a piece of shirt. Jimmie had put the puttee back on, the straps loosened as far as possible. "He thrust and then tried to thrust again in spite of the fact he was wrong end to. So I rapped him over the knuckles with the barrel of my revolver, hard enough to make him drop the knife. The last I saw of your son, his knuckles were skinned a little and he was wearing my gun and belt which I presented to him."

Jimmie told the story as if telling of an amusing incident to a friend. Sahet Khan listened, his eyes holding Jimmie's without wavering.

"Ho! The Great Wolf's cubs are not to be taken without some clawing, no matter how young. Are those that now hold him for you, like you—American?"

"Just the same. I know that the Tartars also love and do not harm children. Learn this, Sahet Khan, the Americans also love and do not harm the little ones. Your son, Zagatai, is an honored guest. Once more, for the Princess Chi Huan, I will trade you your son."

THE GUARD CAME back. "Thy son, Zagatai is not with his mother, Sahet Khan. She has not seen him since last night. No one in the encampment has seen him since last night when he was seen with a Chinese youth. His mother asks that you find him and bring him to her at once."

"Go back and tell her that I will soon put our son in her arms."

After the guard withdrew, Sahet Khan said grimly, "Well for you, American, that the mother of my son lies on a couch of sickness. If she were up she would come seeking her son and being young and hot blooded, might not wait to talk before killing you—as I am doing."

"I'd rather face a dozen Uryankhes Khans than one woman seeking her son," Jimmie answered, with a grin. "Why did you take the Manchu Princess Chi Huan, knowing that all the Manchus in the North would consider the taking a personal insult?"

"I am not afraid of the Manchus in the North or anywhere else, American. Let them come into the hills for me, if they dare. They will remain as food for the jackals and buzzards. I took the Manchu maiden for a Chinese who thinks he is a great war lord. He wishes to force her father to give up territory in exchange for her, he told me. I do not care what he wants to do. I am to get the jade-hilted sword of Genghis Khan, my ancestor, for her. The Chinese found it among some loot hidden away in one of his cities. How it got there is not known. For it I would give all that he could ask and—it may be that if I have you slowly lowered into the boiling oil that before your knees reached the oil those holding my son would release him to save you further torture. Then I would have not only my son but you also."

"It might be," Jimmie answered pleasantly. "Only one thing might interfere. I ordered that whatever was done to me was to be done to your son, Zagatai, and at the same time. I am afraid that before I reached the breaking point, he would be dead. And if I am not seen in the hills, riding towards a certain point with the Princess Chi Huan, it is to be considered that I am dead. Then—thy son grows cold, indeed, oh Khan of the Uryankhes."

Sahet Khan glared at Jimmie for a moment, then grunted. "You win, American. What are jade-hilted swords compared to my son. I will trade. How will the exchange be made?"

"You will ride with the Princess Chi Huan and me with say—fifty riders. Is that sufficient force to withstand attack in the hills?"

"Yes, unless we go too far from the Lower Mountain. All hill people avoid the territory of the Uryankhes and so do the bands of masterless men."

"All right. When we reach a place not far from here I will give the word to halt the escort. You will ride forward with the Princess Chi Huan and me. One man and your son, Zagatai will walk to meet us. You will go back to the riders with your son and I will go with the man and the Princess Chi Huan."

SAHET KHAN DID not like it very much. "What is to stop me, as soon as I have my son back to the riders, from retaking the Manchu maiden, you and the man who comes with you, also? There is a trick."

Jimmie Cordie grinned. "Machine-gun and rifle fire would stop you and fifty Tartars before you got anywhere near us. You know machine guns?"

"Yes. If it had not been for them we would have ridden

over the English at Kota. That stops us charging—but what stops you from taking me?"

"Well—several reasons. The first one being that at the moment we have no special use for a Tartar Khan. What would we do with you after we got you?"

Sahet Khan stared at Jimmie Cordie, then his sense of humor came to the fore. "Ho! Ho! So you have no special use for a Tartar Khan? Truly you Americans are like the English. Once my son is with me and the Manchu maiden with you, what then?"

"Why then all bets are off. That means that either side can do as they see fit. Start something or call it a day and go home."

"It is a trade. I will send for the Manchu maiden and then—we ride, American."

"First I would like to get my leg attended to. From the way it feels it needs looking after."

"I will send for the healers. See, American, it is a game we play during which neither side hurts little ones. This Chinese I took her for has been told to come and get her. He is the one her father drove from Shenshu. I will try to get the sword some other way. After our game is over, come and ride with me. I will show you hill warfare."

"It may be that I will, Sahet Khan. Now I return the Princess Chi Huan to her father."

"Do it and come back. Will you eat and drink?"

"Gladly, after my leg is fixed up."

"I send for the healers, American."

7

"**HERE COMES IT** Jimmie und Chi Huan mit maybeso so—fifty Tartars," announced the Yid from a lookout. Zagatai, who had been fussing around the Browning with Kwang-si, whom he had decided to forgive, came over to the Yid. K'ung had been sent to Meng Wu to tell Prince Chieh that the soldiers of fortune were trying to rescue Chi Huan and where their base was. K'ung was sure he could make it to Meng Wu.

Grigsby, after the arrival of the Yid and Zagatai, had given permission to Kwang-si and Zagatai to fire a few rounds, each to shoot half the ammunition. Afterwards Zagatai, who had looked intently and promptly placed the big white men, demanded that he be allowed to shoot his revolver a few times. Red and the Bean were much better and Red had given Zagatai a lesson in revolver shooting and the Bean had given him a lesson regarding where to hold the hand for a fast draw. So, when the Yid spoke, Zagatai was having the time of his life. So much so that he had promised them that after his father caught them he would ask that they all be slain quickly instead of being flayed or boiled alive in oil.

"It is my father," he said, "also the Manchu maiden and—the one who took me. See, my father rides forward with them. The riders halt and—"

"Come on, Zagatai," Grigsby interrupted. "You are going to your father."

"Ask him to let ye come wid us, ye little half pin devil," Red added. " 'Tis a man we'd make outta ye." He had taken a great fancy to the game little Tartar.

Red spoke in English which Zagatai did not understand but Zagatai grinned just the same. He liked Red very much.

Grigsby smiled as he looked down at Zagatai, swaggering along beside him. Zagatai was hitching his belt around so that his holster would hang at the same angle as Grigsby's.

When they reached the three riders, Jimmie and Chi Huan dismounted. Sahet Khan sat his horse and looked down at his little son. "You spoke the truth, American. My son is unharmed and wears a gun and belt."

"My honorable elder brother always speaks the truth, Tartar," Chi Huan answered haughtily. "Know that from now on."

"I was taken by a trick, Father," Zagatai began as soon as he was close. "See, I have a gun and belt and cartridges. Also I have learned how to shoot a machine gun. When we get one I will be the one to—"

"You are unharmed, little son?"

"Yes, Father. I have been treated with much honor as the son of Sahet Khan. See, this is how you unload the—"

"Mount, cub of the Great Wolf. Your mother awaits you. Show me on the way to her."

"Good-by," Zagatai said, as he mounted the pony Chi Huan had ridden. "Good-by, Manchu maiden. Some day I may come to your city and learn more sword tricks. I have forgiven your cousin for the one he played on me. I will play one on him the first chance I get. Good-by, you who took me. The next time my knife will bite higher up and deeper."

Jimmie grinned as he replied, "Why use your knife, Zagatai? Have you not a gun? Save one of the bullets for me."

Sahet Khan laughed and after a moment, so did Zagatai. "I would use one on you now," he said with Tartar frankness, "only I know that he who stands at your side can draw his gun much faster than I can as yet draw mine."

At that, they all laughed, then Sahet Khan said, "Turn your horse, little son. You have played fair, American. I will remember it. The game is over?"

"Yes, Sahet Khan, the game is over."

"I had intended to at once start another game," Sahet Khan said grimly, "but now—after seeing my son has been treated well—I—"

A WARNING SHOT came from the ledge and also shouts from the riders.

Into the valley from the hills was coming a Chinese regiment with fixed bayonets. Coming fast and from both sides. As they cleared the passes, they spread out into a battle line.

The Chinese war lord had come for the Princess Chi Huan with two regiments of infantry at his back, not trusting Sahet Khan any too much. At the encampment he was told that Sahet Khan had ridden towards the north with her. With his heart filled with a deadly, cold anger, the war lord Tai Chi had started back to his city. On the way, his forward patrols had seen the Tartars riding through the hills. After that report came, Tai Chi and his officers spurred their horses forward, the regiments following at the double. He reached a point from which he could see into the valley just as the Tartars halted.

"Truly the gods smile upon me," he said to his second in command. "Now I will keep the sword of Genghis Khan and also have the Princess Chi Huan. There is Sahet Khan and—it is his son, Zagatai. I will have them also for the Uryankhes to ransom. Order the regiments forward, Liu. The Princess Chi Huan is to be taken alive."

Sahet Khan looked at the Chinese, then said calmly, "We will cut our way through the Chinese mongrels. Good-by, American."

"Good-by," called Zagatai, over his shoulder, his .45 Colt ready for action.

The Tartar escort rode to meet their Khan and his son and then, with Sahet Khan leading and Zagatai flanked on both sides by men of his mother's family, the Tartars charged straight at the nearest Chinese. Chinese marksmanship is very poor and company firing even poorer. The fact that there were fifty odd of the dreaded Uryankhes Tartars charging with raised swords did not improve the Chinese aim at all. In fact, among those of the Chinese that faced the charge, it made it a good deal worse if that were possible.

Sahet Khan and his riders hit the Chinese lines and went through like a sharp knife goes through cheese, without more than two or three saddles being emptied. So much contempt did they have for the Chinese that riders pulled up, jumped off and picked up the wounded Tartars, remounted and came on. The Tartars disappeared in the hills with yells of triumph.

For the moment, the Chinese had given all their attention to the Tartars and while they were doing it, Chi Huan, Jimmie Cordie and Grigsby had made it to the ledge.

A Chinese company started confidently up the slope but had not covered more than a hundred yards before a machine gun opened its staccato, snarling song of death.

The Chinese army slowed up and then after a moment or so, what was left of it, retreated.

8

THE PRINCESS CHI HUAN, as she arrived, had called, "Here I am! Hullo Yid and Beaneater! Red, here I am! Jimmie Cordie rescued me and everything!"

Red swept her up in his brawny arms. "Are you hurted, darlin'? Tell old Red. Did the wildmen hurt ye at all?"

Chi Huan's slim young arms went around Red's neck and her velvet cheek to his rough one, "No, Red. I am all right. Oh, I am so glad to see you, Red dalling. I knew I was rescued when I saw Jimmie in the Tartar dog's tent. When I came in and Jimmie grinned at me, I—"

The machine gun opened up again. Now Jimmie Cordie was behind it with Kwang-si as a helper. Grigsby, the Yid and the Bean were standing about three feet apart at the edge of the ledge, their thirty-thirty rifles sending a sleet of bullets to meet the oncoming Chinese troops.

"Put me down, Red," commanded Chi Huan, "I will tell you all about it, later."

Red was already putting her down and, once on her feet, she ran to the machine gun, beside which she saw a thirty-thirty rifle, The Manchus never bound the feet of the girl babies, as did the Chinese, and Chi Huan's perfect little arched feet carried her to the rifle very fast indeed.

Jimmie Cordie saw her stoop and pick it up and, as Kwang-si was hooking on a belt, tossed her a belt of thirty-thirty cartridges that he had placed near him. "Hop to it, Missee Iron Hat," he said with a grin.

She caught the belt, then announced as she wrapped it twice around her waist, "I am not Missee Iron Hat! The Iron Hats were Chinese as I have told you a hundred times, Jimmie Cordie! I am the Princess Chi Huan of the—"

"So you are. I keep forgetting. That rifle is loaded, mighty Plincess of the Manchus. Watch your step with 'er."

The Manchu Princess Chi Huan made a regular bad little girl's face at Jimmie Cordie, her dainty nose wrinkling up as her tongue came out. After which she ran to the line, getting beside Red.

"Get down and peek over the edge, darlin'," he commanded.

"I won't. Get over a little, Red. I am a very good shot with a rifle."

THE CHINESE CAME up in scattered waves, having learned a lesson about charging company front. It was a hard charge to stop, coming the way it did. One thing that helped a lot to stop it at least for a few minutes was that the men on the ledge were all veterans, all shots and all unafraid. It was a merciless, accurate fire that dropped man after man and finally when about half way up, the Chinese broke and ran back.

The Princess Chi Huan stood there, a delighted smile on her exquisite lips and in her eyes. Here was a fight and she was right up on the firing line. She emptied the rifle and demanded that Red reload it for her.

Tai Chi, watching through his glasses, said as the Chinese ran, "I know now who is with the Princess Chi Huan. It is the men who fought for her father. If they have plenty of ammunition they can drive back anything but a massed charge. Sahet Khan may return soon with the Uryankhes. Order all troops forward, officers leading. The slicing death for the ones who retreat." He did not care how many men he lost. There was always plenty of Chinese to fill his regiments, whether they wanted to become soldiers or not.

Jimmie Cordie looked at the remaining belts of ammunition, then grinned and rose. "You may shoot the remaining belts, Kwang-si. This as a reward for your more than efficient help. And also, so that you may explain to the Chieftains who sit on High how a machine gun works. There is no doubt but what you are going to meet them pronto and in haste."

Chi Huan, as Jimmie came up to the line, silently held out the rifle. It was plain that she did it very much against her will.

"You're doing all right with it, golden one," Jimmie said. "Keep it. I'll fall back on old man Colt's masterpiece. George, I thought I'd give Kwang-si a chance to strut his stuff before he went on High."

Grigsby laughed. "That's the boy, Jeems. This bird, whoever he is, has decided not to fool around any longer. He's coming right up and over this time."

"It looks like it. I wish there were some place that Chi Huan and Kwang-si could start running for, but darned if I can see where they can get off this ledge without being—"

"What, I? Run?" demanded Chi Huan indignantly. "Well, I won't run, Jimmie Cordie. I am not afraid to die. I will stay right here and fight. The Chieftains of the House of Nurhachu who sit on High would hide their faces in their robes for shame if one of their House ran from a fight. You are not to say that I should run, Jimmie Cordie. I am very, very angry with you."

Jimmie grinned. "All right. Stay right here, then. Anyway there is no place to run, darling. How about digging a hole and pulling the hole in after you?"

"I won't! And you are not to tease me, either, I will—"

"They are getting pretty close, Jimmie," the Boston Bean called over.

"We'll let them get up to the rocks," Jimmie answered. "They will have to bunch a little there."

The hard bitten soldiers of fortune watched the steady, slow advance. The Princess Chi Huan also watched, the same kind of a frozen little smile on her lips as was on theirs.

"They march as if well trained," she said, as if watching troops from her palace balcony.

"They are," Jimmie replied. "Trained to know that death is also behind as well as— cut loose, Kwang-si!"

The machine gun instantly responded. As Chi Huan raised her rifle, she said firmly, "The next time I am going to shoot the Browning."

It did not look very much as if there were ever going to be a next time for any of the ledge defenders. After a minute or so, the machine gun stopped and one by one the rifles were dropped and the heavy Colts drawn. In spite of losses, the Chinese came steadily on this time.

"Get behind me, Chi Huan," Jimmie ordered.

"I won't. I wish that my swords were here. They would lessen these pariah curs."

As if by magic, only waiting for the wish to be expressed,

deep wedges of Manchu swordsmen came hurtling down the sides of the hills and from the passes. Behind them came the rifle regiments of Prince Chieh. A bugle sounded in the hills and a mountain battery opened fire. Tai Chi's men were fleeing in every direction that took them away from the Manchus. Tai Chi amid his officers started to flee also but a shell exploded within a foot of his head and he died. Other shells blew many of his officers from their saddles.

The less badly wounded Manchus had made it to Meng Wu from the fight with the Tartars and Prince Chieh had mustered all his forces, leaving only enough men to defend Meng Wu and headed for the Tartar encampment. On the way he had met K'ung. After hearing what K'ung had to tell him, Prince Chieh swung to the right to pick up the soldiers of fortune.

Chi Huan was so surprised at the prompt filling of her wish that she stood with eyes and mouth wide open.

Jimmie Cordie laughed as he holstered his Colt. "Now wish for some ice cream and cake, Missee Iron Hat."

HOW DO YOU SPOKE A GUN?

The Little Manchu Princess Was Very
Anxious to Know How to Spoke a Gun;
and Her Quest for Information Caused
a Lot of Trouble to her "Fliends"

"LET'S GO, YID," the Boston Bean said, as he tightened his finger on the trigger of a thirty-thirty Winchester.

The Fighting Yid opened fire on the advancing Chinese and began to talk as he always did in a fight. "Von for you, mit de Sam Brown belt, und von for—"

The Boston Bean emptied his rifle and tried to reload. He could not make it. His left hand and arm had gone dead on him. The Bean dropped the rifle and with an effort got up on his feet, drawing his .45 Colt.

"O.K. with you, Beany?"

"Perfectly, Mr. Cohen. It's the lucky seventh and I'm up to stretch. I wish the hills would stop spinning around like a top."

"Sit down again and take it easy. Poppa will take it care of the war."

"I will like hell. Since when have I sat down when—when—" the Bean swayed forward, caught himself and came erect again, for a moment, then swayed forward again and this time went all the way down.

The Yid, whose wounds were commencing to bleed once more and whose left leg was entirely out of commission, eased himself over so that he partly covered the Bean's body with his own. "I will stand them off, Codfisher," he said cheerfully. "Take a rest. All is jake with us."

It did not look to be very jake with the Boston Bean and the Fighting Yid. In fact, to coin a word, it looked to be very unjake. The cold gray dawn disclosed the Bean and the Yid sitting back to back on top of a small knoll in the foothills of the T'ian Shan range of mountains, northwest China. They were both wounded, the Bean wearing a bloody bandage set rakishly over his right eye and another around his left forearm.

The Yid's left leg was bandaged and he had two or three sword cuts distributed around that did not amount to much but were painful and bleeding more or less.

The dawn also had disclosed what was left of a company of infantry the war lord San Hsai had sent to capture the two foreign devils who had dared enter his territory. The infantry had waited until dawn for the finals.

THE TWO SOLDIERS of fortune had, by mischance, while hunting for the ruins of a temple under which it was rumored jewels were buried, got too close to San Hsai's walled city. The war lord sent men out to bring the foreign devils in. Objecting to being brought anywhere, knowing full well what would happen to them right afterwards, the Bean and the Yid voiced their objections with a machine gun and what rifles and whatnot their bearers had along. But the war lord's men outnumbered them and wiped out the army of the Bean and Yid. Also they would have got the two foreign devils if, at last, the Bean and the Yid had not executed what the Japs call a rearward movement, commonly known in other circles as a retreat.

There then began a game of tag in the hills. The tagging being done with bullets and swords. The Bean and the Yid very soon demonstrated the fact that if a Chinese infan-

tryman got lined up with their, the Bean and the Yid's, rifle sights, he became a dead infantryman. So it became a game of ambush and counter ambush. Once, by sheer chance, the Bean and the Yid ran smack into a party of ten or twelve of the war lord's men who were seeking to get to the right of them.

The two utterly reckless soldiers of fortune fought their way through but in doing it, got wounded in several places. They made their way to the top of the knoll but once there, could go no farther. The thought of surrender never entered either of their minds.

The Bean did not answer the Yid's "all is jake with us" and the Yid began shooting and talking again, as man after man of the advance went down under his deadly rifle. The Chinese had evidently decided to put a period to the party. They were going to come up the knoll and if possible take the Bean and the Yid prisoners, if not, kill them, all losses to the contrary notwithstanding. And it looked very much as though they were going to succeed in doing that very thing.

"And one for you with the officer's cap. My, you are getting close to the—what the hell now?"

Out of a pass came a detachment of Chinese cavalry. The attacking force saw it as soon as the Yid did. As one man, they ran for the hills. The first look had been sufficient to tell them that in the excitement of the game they had got a little too far away from home and into the territory of another war lord who would just as soon boil them in oil as not; in fact, a little rather. Their war lord and this one were at sword's point and woe betide the man of one the other caught.

"Hey, Beany! Wake up! We got company. The infantry is running and the—Beany, wake up! Something is doing. Here comes an officer with a flag of truce."

THE BEAN BLINKED his eyes and then slowly sat up, just as a Chinese officer pulled up his horse about ten feet away and announced in Pushtu, the universal language of the border, "I come as a friend. I am Captain Leng-Lu, of the war lord Kwangsi's army. Lower your rifle and—"

"Dismount," the Bean interrupted, "Who are you to sit

and overlook us? Dismount or I will shoot you out of that saddle."

"Oi, Codfish! Wait, I ask you. Flag of truce! Beany, put up the gat."

"I don't see any—any— I don't see any—" The Bean fell back, this time absolutely out of commission.

The Chinese officer dismounted. "I meant no insult. You are he who is called The Fighting Yid?"

"That's right, I am the Fighting Yid. Say what you got to say with the well known snap. I am about to enter the—" The Yid saw that the officer did not understand English and so said "Yes" in Pushtu.

"And this other man is The Boston Bean?"

"Yes."

"You fought the machine guns for the war lord Chai?"

"Yes and the big guns also. Be quick. I am entering the darkness."

"The lord Kwangsi was told that you were in the hills fighting off a pack of curs who snarled at your heels. He sent me to bring you to him, having guns for you to fight."

"Well, well. We were just going to shut up shop and call it a day when along comes a customer. Order litters be made to carry us and—" The Yid fell across the Bean, not realizing he had once more spoken in English.

IN THE WALLED city of Chaoking, held by the Manchu prince Chieh-yu, it was known that Kwangsi, war lord of Lukshun, had received some heavy guns from the south and was mounting them in the hills to shell Chaoking. Kwangsi was ambitious to control that neck of the woods and in addition to fighting the war lord San Hsai decided that he was strong enough to try for Chaoking—at the same time. But he soon found out that to take a walled city defended by Manchus and by machine guns manned by American soldiers of fortune was not to be done off hand. His troops had been driven back by machine gun and rapid fire guns every time they advanced against the walls. At last Kwangsi decided that before he ordered another charge he would get some big guns and knock the walls of Chaoking into a cocked hat.

Ten days after the Bean and the Yid had been carried to Lukshun, the little Manchu Princess Wu-Tze, only child of Prince Chieh-yu, sat down on a bag of sand near where Red Dolan was directing the removal of some rapid fire guns to a less exposed position.

"Hullo, Led," she said sociably, in English, "Ale you getting leady to leceive the monglels who will come to die befole our walls?"

Wu-Tze, aged fifteen, looked in her bright silks like an exotic lovely tropical flower. She may have looked like one but as Red Dolan—ex Foreign Legion and lieutenant of military police, A.E.F., two hundred and twenty-odd pounds of red-headed fighting Irish—said:

"Inside, Herself is ten wildcats and wan hundred and ten grizzly bears all rolled together." It was Mr. Dolan's way of stating that the little princess was a natural born scrapper. She was, to the marrow of her bones. In her veins there flowed the blood of the chieftains who had cut their way with the sword to the Peacock throne of China.

"Yes, darlin'. These guns are goin' above the gate. With me and Jimmie and George and Carewe to fight them, 'tis few of the di-ert-ty scuts of the world will get within callin' distance. They'll think that all hell has—I beg the pardon of ye, alanna." To Red, little Wu-Tze was "Herself" and woe betide the one who crossed her.

"It it glanted, Led. It is war time and we are not in my flower galdens where language must be guarded. I am vely glad that you, my honorable elder blothers, are here to fight for my mighty father."

Prince Chieh-yu had, at one time, been first secretary to the Chinese Embassy, Washington, and Wu-Tze had gone to school there. Her English was very good, save for the fatal "r." There is no "r" in the Chinese language and few Chinese can make a sound like it. The Manchus have spoken Chinese for the last two hundred years, their own language having been discarded for some unknown reason. An "l" is substituted for the "r" unless it comes at the end of a word—then it can be managed, once in a while, by educated Manchus or Chinese who have been educated abroad. But if starting a word or surrounded by other letters, very, very seldom.

Prince Chieh-yu, when he knew he was in for a war with Kwangsi, had sent for some soldiers of fortune who had fought for him before, to come up and help him show Kwangsi, who was topside man. Jimmie Cordie, ex-sergeant Foreign Legion and captain of machine gun company A.E.F., Red Dolan, George Grigsby, ex Foreign Legion with Jimmie and Red and Major of Infantry, A.E.F.; John Carewe, ex Flight Commander of a British air squadron and several other American and English adventurers, had responded. Wu-Tze had known Jimmie Cordie, Red Dolan, Grigsby and Carewe since she was eight years old. At first she looked them over and studied them for a week or more. Then she gravely announced that they were "her honorable elder brothers," to be honored and obeyed as such by all who wished to remain healthy, or words to that effect. The hard-bitten soldiers of fortune grinned and promptly accepted Wu-Tze as one of themselves. If she had a favorite it was the big red-headed Irishman, Red Dolan.

"I wish," she went on, "that the Beaneater and the Yid had come, also. Why didn't they, Red? They always said that they loved me."

"So they do, darlin'. They both love ye like the dickens an' all. When the word came they was off huntin' for jewels somewhere—the benighted monkey-faced baboons."

MOST OF THE time, the Bean and the Yid were with Jimmie Cordie and the others who made up what was called in the Orient, "Jimmie Cordie's outfit."

"Then they do not know that we are being attacked by this cur Kwangsi. If they did they would be here. I wish the jackal would put the test to the sword. Manchu swords would very soon lesson him. He is aflaid to do it, Red. That reminds me, how do you spoke a gun?"

"How do I what? Ye mean fire a gun, darlin'?" Jimmie Cordie, slim, wiry, black-eyed, thin-faced and tight-lipped, came up and sat down on a sand bag. "Hello. Missee Iron Hat. Are you holding a council of war with General Dolan?"

"I am not Missee Iron Hat," Wu-Tze answered promptly, "And you know it, Jimmie Cordie. I am the Princess Wu-Tze of the House of Tze and of the Sin-ka-ing Clans. The Iron Hats were Chinese who helped the Manchus con—"

"By gosh, that's right. I keep forgetting it, I remember now that you are not Missee Iron Hat."

"Quit teasin' Herself," Red commanded. "Ye know full well, ye shrimp, that Herself is no Iron Hat."

"Jimmie is not teasing me, Red. It is a joke between us," Wu-Tze stated, with a smile. "Jimmie always calls me that and I always tell him that—"

"Now you know the truth, Mr. Dolan, get over on the south wall and give Carewe a hand." Jimmie Cordie was second in command for Chieh-yu.

"I'm on the way. Herself just asked me how to spoke a gun—whatever that is," Red said, as he started.

"How to what? I never heard of spoking—oh, you mean spiking a gun, Wu-Tze?"

"None of your business, Jimmie Cordie. I don't have to tell you."

"The heck it isn't some of my business. I know you full well, Missee Iron Hat. Any old time you show interest in things of war, the said interest is open to suspicion. How come this wanting to know how to spike a gun, oh mighty Manchu Princess?"

"I have just told you that it is none of your business," answered Wu-Tze hotly. "I do not have to explain my interests to you."

"That's right, you don't, when all is said and done. All right, from now on, you keep away from the machine guns."

"What? I won't. How dare you order me to do anything? I will stay around the machine guns all I wish and—and—" Wu-Tze stopped talking. She knew that any order given by Jimmie Cordie would promptly be backed up by her father. And if there was one thing she loved to do, that thing was to get as close as she could to a machine gun and, if she could coax the gunner, fire it for a few bursts. Red had taught her the mechanism and let her fire his gun when they were establishing range and cross fire. Another thing that made her stop talking was the fact that she thought a lot of Jimmie Cordie. So she weakened, something she seldom did under any circumstances.

"I—I am sorry I spoke like that, Jimmie darling. I know that if you give the order I must stay away from the guns."

"That's a good girl. I withdraw the order. Now, as one machine gun expert to another, what is this gun spiking thing?"

"Why—why—once I read in history that some volunteers went out of a fort and spoked—I mean spiked—the enemies' guns. So I thought that if we—"

A MANCHU OFFICER came up and saluted. "Prince Chieh-yu's compliments and will Captain Cordie join him at the west gate."

"I'll go with you, Liang. You forget about that gun spiking, Madame the Plincess," the last to Wu-Tze.

The little Wu-Tze smiled at him but as Jimmie remembered later, did not answer.

What she did do, as soon as Jimmie was out of sight, was to hunt up her cousin T'ang and go into deep conference. T'ang, who was a year older than Wu-Tze and very much like her, thought the idea she advanced a fine one. At the finish of the conference she said, "We will gain much honor and our names will be engraved in the golden book of the House of Tze. Pick out those of the School of Swords that you deem worthy of going with us." After that she found Carewe, who told her what spiking a gun meant and how, as far as he knew, to do it. Carewe did not have any idea what the little Princess was asking, save for general information.

THE WAR LORD Kwangsi sat in one of the smaller audience rooms in his palace at Lukshun. Captain Leng-Lu stood at attention before the dais.

"You have my permission to speak, Captain."

"The foreign devils are now well enough to go to the guns, Lord of the North."

"Take them there and have them test elevation and range. Promise them what they ask. Once the guns have opened fire and it is proved they are correct, slay them both. We will not need them further."

"As you order, Ruler of the World."

The Yid, as Kwangsi was calmly ordering that the Bean and the Yid be slain, sat on the edge of the Bean's couch. The Bean was half sitting up, propped up with cushions.

"How you feelin' now, Codfisher?"

The Bean, named in the Massachusetts Social Register as John Cabot Winthrop, and called in the Orient anything that had the remotest connection to his birthplace, Boston, grinned as he answered, "All right. That doctor sure knows his stuff." The Bean was long, lean and lanky, with a sorrowful, woebegone look. It was very misleading, that look. He was happy-go-lucky and reckless to the nth degree. Once a former Texas Ranger, while the Bean was under discussion, remarked, "He is a very regardless jasper." Being an ex-ranger, he felt qualified to pass on regardless jaspers. The Codfish Duke of Massachusetts had served in the Foreign Legion with Jimmie Cordie, Red Dolan and George Grigsby and in the A.E.F. as captain of artillery.

"If you mean the stuff he rubbed in the vounds, he sure does. My, such nice smelling stuff. Two rubs and the cuts healed. He said that he graduated from the London Hospital." The Yid, who was about as broad as he was long, born on Hester Street, New York, had been Jimmie Cordie's first sergeant in France. His china blue eyes seemed always to be popping out of his head with surprise at such goings on in a naughty old world. It was as misleading a look as the Bean's sorrowful one. The Yid was never surprised at anything and also, would fight anything, at any time, any place, regardless of odds—and have a perfectly fine time while doing it. Hence his nickname, "The Fighting Yid."

"Have you found out who we are going to blow off the map?"

"Sure. The doctor told me. The Prince Chieh-yu."

"What? The Little Wu-Tze's pa? My sainted Aunt Maria!"

"That's him."

"For Pete's sake! I didn't think we were within fifty miles of Chaoking. Listen, you Yid ape, we can't fight him. Jimmie would raise hell and high water. We've fought for Prince Chieh-yu."

"What difference does that make?" asked the Yid cheerfully. "They all look alike to me."

"Yeah? Well, they don't to me, Mister Cohen. Nothing doing. I'll train no guns on Chaoking and that's that."

"Oi, such a business. Wait a minute, I ask you. We was down and all in and out when this war lord rescued us, didn't he? Well, now we are well and—"

"Did you promise to fight the guns for him at that time?"

"I don't remember wot I said. The officer say something and I answer. I remember that. Then I went to sleep."

"Well, I don't give two hoots in hell what you said. You can do as you see fit. What I am going to do is to get the heck out of here and make it to Chaoking. If I do make it, I'll turn a machine gun on you with the greatest of pleasure, also bullets, my fair friend from Hester Street."

THE YID GRINNED, "You and me is pardners, ain't we? I go with you, Beaneater. What do I care for this Chink?"

"Where are our guns?"

"The .45s are over there in the corner with our belts. What happened to the rifles, I don't know."

"We'll try for Chaoking. Ethics and ethics and all this. This war lord may have saved our lives but I don't fight against Prince Chieh-yu for all the double damned ethics in the world."

"I never had them."

"You never had what?"

"I never had it them ethics you are talking about. Are they like smallpox?"

"Are they—get the hell out of here, you Yid nitwit. I want to think."

"Beany, listen. We pretend that we set up the guns and when night comes we sneak through the lines and—"

Captain Leng-Lu came in. "You are well enough to go to the guns?"

"Yes," answered the Bean, getting up from the couch, "we are well enough, Captain."

Captain Leng-Lu voiced no objection as the Yid and the Bean buckled on the belts from which hung the holstered .45 Colts. He probably thought that it made no difference.

Shots in the back would send the two foreign devils to their special hell before they had time to draw their guns.

Once at the place the guns were being placed they were given a tent and instructed to see to it that the guns had the proper elevation and range. It was about eleven o'clock that night when the Yid entered the tent. The Bean had been in for an hour or so.

"Well," the Yid said, with a grin, "now I know we got to take it on the well known lam, ain't we? I just got through with the elevation and I bet you I made a big mistake with the figures you gave me. I bet you the shells fly away over Chaoking. Oi, how could it be I was so careless?"

CAPTAIN LENG-LU ENTERED the tent. "I am going to stay here with you gentlemen, if you will permit," he announced politely. "I wish to see the guns open in the morning."

"Glad to have you," answered the Bean. "Make yourself at home. Try some of that wine Colonel Kai so kindly sent us."

The Chinese captain smiled and sat down, little knowing that he was as close to his death as he could be and meet it. The Yid and the Bean knew that, if they wanted to make Chaoking, their visitor would have to be disposed of; and in the disposing of persons who stood in their way, the Yid and the Bean were apt to be careless of human life.

"You will both receive much gold," Leng-Lu started, "after the city of Chaoking has been taken. The war lord—"

A voice from outside called, "Captain Leng-Lu! We have a prisoner here. Colonel Kai ordered her brought to you, the staff officer of Lord Kwangsi." Incidentally, the colonel had taken one look at the prisoner and at once decided that he had much rather have a staff officer attend to the matter. He personally wanted no Manchu blood feud on his hands.

"If you permit, I will order the prisoner brought in here," Leng-Lu said to the Bean and the Yid.

"Please treat this tent as your own," the Bean answered politely.

"Bring the prisoner in here," called Leng-Lu.

Into the tent came two soldiers, then the Princess Wu-Tze, her hands tied behind her back, a gag in her mouth, then two more soldiers.

Captain Leng-Lu's eyes widened as he saw her, and inwardly he cursed Colonel Kai for passing the buck to him. A Manchu princess of the blood was a very dangerous lady for any Chinese captain to have in his charge.

"Unbind her hands and remove the gag," he ordered and after the order had been obeyed, "Out! The matter of the reward will be taken up in the morning."

Wu-Tze, once the gag had been taken out of her mouth, drew a long breath. As she was doing it, she saw the Yid and the Bean. The Yid was standing to the left and a little behind Captain Leng-Lu. The Bean, who was shoulders and head taller than the Chinese officer, was to the right of the Yid, and in a position to put a finger to his lips without Leng-Lu seeing it.

WU-TZE, WHO WAS as fast mentally as she was physically, absolutely ignored the two foreign devils. She glared at Captain Leng-Lu, who bowed very low. "You bow to me, jackal? When your curs have dared to defile my mouth with an unclean rag? My father will boil you in oil, descendant of mongrels." This in Mandarin Chinese.

The fact that her sortie to spike the guns had failed—

that she alone remained alive of those whom had come
with her, her cousin included, and that she was a prisoner
in the hands of one of the most merciless and cruel war
lords of all China, made no difference. She had been taken,
bound and gagged and then thrown over a shoulder as if
a sack of grain. Any one of the several things would have
unleashed her temper; all of them combined made the
little Manchu like an angry wolverine. That the Yid and
the Bean were there and would help her, she knew. But at
the moment, she was strictly on her own.

Captain Leng-Lu did not at all like the reference to his
ancestors or the tone of her voice, either. But he knew that
the fortunes of war were uncertain and it was within the
range of possibilities that Prince Chieh-yu could make
his daughter's promise come true. He also knew that all
Manchus, in the North or any other place, would resent
an insult to the Princess Wu-Tze. Being captured in open
warfare was one thing—and an insult to her person was
most distinctly another.

So he answered, "I regret that those who took you, oh
Manchu princess of the blood, did not honor you as your
exalted rank demands. They will be taught the error of
their ways. I will order that clear water and other things
be brought you at once. Then an honor guard will escort
you to the Lord Kwangsi. I ask your protection when your
mighty father questions my connection with the matter of
your capture. Know, oh resplendent lotus bud, that I am
but a lowly captain and as you know must obey orders. I—"

He pitched forward, to be caught and lowered to the
ground by the Yid. The Boston Bean's Colt barrel had hit

him in the back of his neck, sending him down like a poled ox falls, without even a sobbing breath.

"Keep right on talking, Wu-Tze," the Bean commanded calmly. "Tell him some more about his relations. Loud, so that those outside can hear you."

WU-TZE SMILED, FOR the first time since she had seen the young swordsmen of the School of Swords go down under Chinese bayonets. This was action and she responded to it at once.

"You and the low caste sons of unspeakable mothers, who have dared to touch me, will die many deaths before your foul spirits go howling out into the cold darkness. You have touched the person of a Manchu princess of the blood and—"

"Come on," the Bean commanded, "get busy, you Hester Street ape. Get his clothes off. Keep it up, Wu-Tze. And while you're doing it, get into these clothes."

Three minutes later, the Bean and the Yid and what looked like, at least from a distance, Captain Leng-Lu, came out of the tent.

"Keep between us, Wu-Tze," the Bean ordered. "That uniform fits you kind of sudden in places."

It looked, for a minute or two, as if they were going to get by with it and make the hills. Then an officer stepped from the shadows. "You go beyond the lines, Captain Leng-Lu?"

"I go where I please," snarled back Wu-Tze, in a very good imitation of Captain Leng-Lu's voice. "Go back to your post and—"

The Nine Red Gods must have decided that things were too easy for the escaping party, because they sent a little puff of wind and brought the moon out from behind a cloud. The wind lifted Captain Leng-Lu's cap from the head of Wu-Tze. It being about four sizes too large for her. The moon enabled the Chinese officer to see clearly. "You are not Captain Leng-Lu! To me, men of—" He was drawing his gun when the Yid shot him dead.

"To the right! To the right! We shoot our way through! Around the guns, Beany."

Chinese soldiers came up from all sides. All they knew at the moment was that it looked as if one of the foreign devils had shot an officer and that Captain Leng-Lu was with the foreign devils. They saw the guns in the hands of the Yid and the Bean and without knowing what it was all about, started to close in.

"Let 'em have it," the Bean commanded calmly. "Get to the cement bags, Yid. We can hold 'em off for a— quit that, you little bobcat."

Wu-Tze had run to the body of the officer and drawn his sword from the sheath. "Now," she announced triumphantly, "I have something to fight with."

She did not have a chance to use the sword, at least for the moment. The deadly guns of the Yid and the Bean cleared the way to the gun placements where there were a good many bags of cement and timbers that had not been used.

AS THEY REACHED their goal and got behind the bags and timber, the yells of the Chinese stopped and they heard a voice snarling orders. It was the voice of Kwangsi, who had come to look over the big guns before they opened fire in the morning.

"Oi," the Yid said, "de main squeeze is here in person. Now ve catch hell, no fooling."

"What do you care? We've got a fort, haven't we? My, what a dirty face you've got, Wu-Tze." The Boston Bean was running true to form, as ever.

"My face is not dirty! Your face would be dirty too if you had been—my mouth and tongue taste very bad and—and—" Her dainty lips began to quiver, in spite of her effort to keep them straight. After all, Wu-Tze was only a little girl even if she were a Manchu princess of the blood.

"Wait," the Yid said hastily. "I got some brandy. Here, rinse your mouth with this, darling. Then take a drink. That's a good girl. Now wash your face in it. The Beaneater is no good and also—"

The Bean's gun detonated and a soldier fell over the bags. The war lord Kwangsi had ordered his men to bring to him the Manchu princess and the two foreign devils, unhurt.

Other soldiers appeared over the bags. The Yid and the Bean did the best they could, which was very good and the little Manchu princess stood to it manfully with her sword, but there were too many of the Chinese. The moon came out, making it almost as light as day.

Five minutes later the Bean and the Yid lay pegged out on the ground and Wu-Tze stood in front of Kwangsi.

"You mongrels of America will die very slowly. Colonel Kai, take the Manchu Princess Wu-Tze to Lukshun."

"My mighty father will lesson you, Chinese dog! He will—"

"But in the meantime, I have you. It may be that he will give up his—"

The sound of distant gunfire came plainly. "Chieh-yu attacks! Weng, bring up your regiments! Hoi, lead your men forward! Colonel Kai, take the Princess Wu-Tze to the rear and guard her. Wong, support Weng with your regiment."

The gunfire steadily became louder. Colonel Kai listened for a moment as Kwangsi and his staff rode away. He had no desire to meet a Manchu sword charge in the open and he knew that his men would not meet it. He decided that he and his regiment would be far better off if they started south from where they stood—and acted on his decision, promptly. He ran towards the guns, shouting orders, ignoring the little Manchu princess.

SHE RAN TO where the Bean and the Yid lay, their arms and legs stretched out as far as they would go, tied to pegs driven in the ground. Their faces looked up into the blue.

"My resplendent father comes," she announced. "See. From the hills there comes a line of bayonets and swordsmen. I knew he—"

"Oi, how can we see, darling? Untie us and— get down!"

Machine gun bullets came close, very close. As if they were erecting a steel fence around Wu-Tze—which they were.

"I won't get down. I—"

"What the hell is—that's Jimmie Cordie and Red Dolan shooting. I know the vay they can make a—"

"Get down, Wu-Tze," commanded the Bean. "You may get hit if you—well, you darned bobcat."

Wu-Tze, instead of getting down, had climbed up on a rock. "Why should I get down? Oh! Here comes Jimmie and Red and Carewe and—and Grigsby with the machine guns and my mighty father with the rifle regiments and the swords! The mongrel's regiments go to meet them. The swords charge and—and— Oh, brave swords! They cut their way through. Now, how do you like Manchu sword-play, Chinese jackals? Two rifle regiments come from the west and—and more swords from the pass. They are—are— see, the School of Swords advance! They are— yes, they are through the curs and—brave swords! Brave swords! I wish I were there to lead them and—"

"Hey, listen," coaxed the Yid. "Untie it us, darling. Then we can get in the fight."

"Oh, my gracious! I forgot all about untying you. I will— right away and— Jimmie! Red! Here we are! Here we are!"

Jimmie Cordie and Red Dolan could do no more than wave to the little Manchu princess for the next five minutes or so, then Red came up. "Are ye hurted, darlin'? Tell old Red. Have the dish-faced scuts put a hand on ye? A hunter came in and told of seein' ye get caught. Out we came wid all the pa ave ye had to take ye back from—from—holy mother! 'Tis the Yid and the Bean! What the hell and all are ye two apes doin' here?"

"Less talking and more untying, Irish bummer. We are—"

"I've a mind to let ye stay there, ye Hester Street scut. Wait till I find me knife."

Red was just finishing the cutting loose of the Yid and the Bean, when Jimmie Cordie came up. "Are you all right, Wu-Tze? Well, if isn't Mr. Cohen and Mr. Winthrop. How come you thusly, gents?"

"Yes, I am all right, Jimmie. But—but—when I think of the brave young swords who have gone on high because I tried to spike some guns, I—I—"

Red swept her up in a pair of brawny arms. "Sure now, darlin', 'tis fighting men they was and what better could happen to fightin' men than to die fightin' for you? See, here comes the pa ave ye to hold ye tight in the arms ave him."

ON THE WAY back to Chaoking, the Bean and the Yid were carried in litters. They had to be, because before they went down they had both taken an awful beating from gun butts and sword hilts.

Red walked between the litters. "What was ye doin' there wid Kwangsi?" he asked.

"When we heard that you vos with Prince Chieh-yu," the Yid answered, "we come up on the run to set the guns so that they would blow off the head of all Irish bummers."

"Well, ye Yid polecat! After us rescuin' ye and all. Sorry the day we ever—"

The Boston Bean raised himself to a sitting position and asked sleepily, "Who opened the cage door and let that red-headed ape out? Go on oway, Terance Aloysius, me good man. You are disturbing my rest."

THOSE THAT LIVE BY THE SWORD

*In which the China coast gives up
a secret—grudgingly, but—*

1

THE JAPANESE MILITARY intelligence headquarters. Harbin, Manchukuo, received a code message from an intelligence officer in the field. Decoded, it read:

> The following Big Swords have left the encampment in the T'ian Shan range and are heading south and east with three hundred Big Sword cavalry as escort. James Cordie, second in command of the Big Swords. George Grigsby, in command of artillery. John Winthrop, known as the "Boston Bean." Terrance Dolan, known as "Red" Dolan. Abraham Cohen, known as the "Fighting Yid." John Carewe, Englishman. The last four named command the machine and rapid-fire guns. They go for ammunition. As soon as they reach Uzbeg territory I will take them with the aid of Uzheg Khan and bring them to Harbin.

As the message was read to the intelligence officers in Harbin, they looked at each other and smiled. Cruel little smiles of anticipation. Once they had the Big Sword officers who had many times tricked and flouted them, they would exact full payment.

But the next message that came wiped the smiles off their faces and demonstrated once more the folly of counting chickens before hatching. It read:

Uzbeg Khan and many tribesmen slain. Will endeavor to
take men mentioned in first message south of the river Tarim.
The cavalry escort is practically wiped out.

After the Japanese colonel in command of intelligence
read the second message, he cursed all intelligence men in
the field and added a few remarks regarding the fighting
ability of the Uzbegs.

A staff officer, recently arrived from Nippon, laughed
and then asked, "Why should the taking or not taking of
a few soldiers of fortune make you so angry, colonel?"

"You do not know these men, Lieutenant General
Choshi. Before they joined the Big Swords we easily
controlled the situation in the west. They brought modern
guns with them and a knowledge of hill fighting we find
hard to combat. With them eliminated, the Big Swords are
a negligible factor. With them, the Big Swords are truly a
thorn in our side."

"I see. If there is anything I can do to help you take them,
let me know. Now, in regards to that matter of—"

Other messages came to the effect that the Big Sword
officers had arrived at this place and that. The last message
was to the effect that they had reached Shanghai, coming
through Honan, aided by the war lord T'ang Lu.

The colonel, Nagaya, read them one by one, his face and
eyes grim and cold. After the last one, he sent a message to
the Japanese intelligence in Shanghai that made the entire
staff there drop all other business.

"DIDN'T I TELL you to stay in bed, you Yid monkey
beneath notice?" demanded Red Dolan, as the Fighting

Yid came into the living room of an apartment on The Bubbling Wells Road, Shanghai.

The Yid's wound was not serious but the doctor had ordered him to keep off his feet as much as possible. And the Yid promptly disobeyed, also as much as possible.

"Vy should I stay it in bed, Irish bummer?" demanded the Yid, who had a bath robe on over his pajamas. "I am vell enough to kick de slats out of all de Dolans mit von foot."

The Yid appeared to be about as broad as he was long and his china-blue eyes always seemed to be popping out of his head with surprise at such naughty doings in a bad old world.

It was very misleading, that surprised look. The Yid was never surprised at anything. And he would fight anything, anywhere and at any time, regardless of odds; hence his name, the Fighting Yid.

"What? You couldn't do that if you was twenty-one times as well, you Hester Street bum of the world." Red Dolan answered promptly.

It might be that the Yid couldn't, at that. Red was two hundred and twenty pounds of fighting Irish, ex-Foreign Legion and lieutenant of military police, A.E.F.

"For Pete's sake, Yid, go back to bed," a long, lean, sorrowful-looking man said, putting down his cards. "You are gumming up the game." A poker game had been in progress when the Yid appeared.

"Deal it me a hand. Beany. I am vell enough to give you suckers a lesson in de playing of—"

A slim, wiry, black-eyed man came in the room just as the Boston Bean was going to interrupt the Yid.

"Well, she's loaded, gents. Twenty thousand rifles and

bayonets. Fifty odd one- and two-pound rapid-fire guns. One hundred machine guns, four mountain batteries and ammunition enough to last us from now until the second coming. We sail for the north in the morning. Any of you birds that want to get anything, now is the time to do 'er."

"My word," a slight, boyish-looking man said. "I have several things to get. Cash me in, Red." He was John Cecil Carewe, former flight commander of a British air squadron, now soldier of fortune in the Orient.

"The Bean's yacht is loaded to the guard rails and then some. 'Eavens 'elp the poor woiking goil if we run into bad weather on the way up," Jimmie Cordie, ex-sergeant Foreign Legion and captain of machine-gun company A.E.F. went on, with a grin.

"The Bean is liable to be minus a perfectly good yacht, what, what, what?" Carewe announced as he counted his chips.

"What's a few yachts here and there?" asked the Boston Bean, mournfully. "I'll answer my own question: Not a darn thing."

The Bean, who was listed in the Massachusetts social register as John Cabot Winthrop, was reckless and happy-go-lucky to the nth degree, in spite of that sorrowful look, which was as misleading as the Yid's surprised one. He had served in the Foreign Legion with Jimmie Cordie, Red Dolan and George Grigsby and in the A.E.F. as captain of artillery.

" 'Tis not your yacht, you long-legged piece of Bosting tripe," Red stated. " 'Tis the yacht of herself and well you know it. Now where're you at, Codfish?"

"Exactly the same place I was before, Terrance Aloysius, me good man. What is mine is mine and what is Mrs. Winthrop's is mine also."

"If Katherine were here, you know darn well she'd say go ahead and take it, you big red-headed ape," Jimmie Cordie added. "Since when have you been—"

"Who is a big red-headed ape?" called a gay voice from the doorway. "Not my dear Red Dolan, I hope."

All the men rose as Katherine Neville Winthrop entered. She was blond, slim and lovely, with the patrician loveliness of a thoroughbred Englishwoman.

"I was lonesome in England," she went on, as she advanced on the Bean, "so I decided to go back to China and—" The rest of the sentence was not finished. She had reached the Boston Bean.

To the strictly reared English girl the soldiers of fortune were a joy forever and she stoutly maintained she loved them all—John the most, of course. The Bean and the Yid had, some three years before, rescued her from Chinese bandits and once she had married the Bean, Katherine became one of the outfit.

The Nevilles had fought England's battles for a thousand years, one of them putting out to fight the great Spanish Armada in a fishing sloop armed with a one-pound brass cannon. From the top of her proudly held head to the tips of her little toes, she was a fighting Neville and the soldiers of fortune knew it. They accepted her as one of themselves and whenever possible, she was with them.

Quite a little later, she said: "I was going to send word to the north that I had arrived in Shanghai but I passed the yacht coming in and Lady Cavendish, whom I met

*The yacht touched the HoYang. "Boarders
away! We take this pirate dog."*

at the dock, told me you were all here. Tell me all about
everything."

They told her of the fighting in the north and of their
coming to Shanghai for guns and ammunition. She
listened, her hyacinth-blue eyes shining, and when it came
to the using of the yacht, answered promptly: "Why, of
course we will take it. It is the only thing to do. We can—"

"Wait a minute, Mrs. Winthrop," the Bean interrupted.
"Did I hear you say 'we'? You should have said 'you' can
take it. By any chance do you think you are going to be
included in gun running off the coast of China and up
rivers? There are nine thousand and eight Jap warships of
various sizes that—"

"Why, John Cabot Winthrop! Do you mean to sit there and try to tell me I am not going? Well, I guess I am going. George, say that I am. I will agree to come back to Shanghai on the yacht after the unloading but I am going that far."

George Grigsby, a man fully as big and strong as Red Dolan, ex-Foreign Legion and major of infantry A.E.F., smiled. "Better stay here, Katherine. It is touch and go—mostly touch, running the gauntlet of Jap ships all the way up."

The argument that followed raged for half an hour. Red, the Yid and Katherine on one side—the "I go" side—and the Bean, Jimmie Cordie, Carewe and Grigsby on the "Oh, no you don't" side.

At last Katherine fired the shot that sank the opposition. "Very well. The *Katherine* is my yacht. If I cannot go, neither can the *Katherine*. You can start to unload her, Jimmie Cordie."

At that, Jimmie grinned. "All right, Mrs. Codfish. Come right along—and get blown out of the water with the rest of us. You win."

"I fully intend to."

The Bean, Carewe and Grigsby agreed that the Neville had won.

2

MAJOR TOTA, JAPANESE military intelligence, entered the private office of a supposed merchant. Another Japanese officer rose and saluted.

"The *Katherine* sails at dawn," Major Tota said, curtly, after he had returned the salute and sat down. "Be seated, Captain Yatsu. On board her are the ones we want and also an Englishwoman, wife of the Boston Bean. We will use the *HoYang*."

"The *HoYang?* I do not understand, major."

"There is no reason why you should, captain. Your work has not brought you here in Shanghai with us until recently. I will tell you of the *HoYang*, but first— You are of the Tokugawa shoguns?"

"Yes. I am entitled to display the banner bearing the circle with the three asarum leaves, Major Tota."

"Swear then, on the honor of the Tokugawa, that what I tell you is to be held by you in strictest confidence."

"I swear it on the honor of the Tokugawa."

"The *HoYang* was, at one time, a tramp steamer. She was captured by pirates and used by them. A little later she was taken to a sheltered bay and there remodeled. Powerful engines were put in her and six four-inch rifles mounted on her berth deck. They cannot be seen until run out to be fired. She also has lighter guns on her spar deck, also concealed."

"But—how do you know this, major? You say that she belongs to pirates."

"I said she did. Now she belongs to us of the intelligence. I will not go into details at the moment. We have found her very useful. Many ships belonging to different nationalities carrying munitions to Chinese war lords who fight us, have been sunk by the pirate craft, *HoYang*. Now do you see?"

"Yes—but who mans her?"

"The Chinese pirate who took her. There are several Nipponese gunners on board who, sad to relate, have turned pirate. The Chinese receives from us, in addition to the loot he is allowed to keep, so much gold per month. The *HoYang* will sink the yacht of the Boston Bean and the mongrels we are after."

"But—why cannot one of our destroyers do that? She is carrying arms to the Big Swords who—"

"Could we prove that? She carries the American flag. Shall one of our destroyers fire on the flag of the Yankee bluffers? Not yet, Captain Yatsu. Fishing boats or other craft might be within seeing distance when the *Katherine* is sunk. What have we of Nippon to do with a pirate attack on an American vessel?"

"That is correct, major. But—can the *HoYang* catch the *Katherine*, once the latter is at sea? The American yachts are known to be very fast."

"So is the *HoYang* very fast. Once more I will tell you something in strict confidence. I have a man who does as I order or—hangs for murder in Tokyo. I think he will sail on the *Katherine.* If he does, we will have no trouble in crossing her bow. If he does not—there are other ways."

"You say 'we cross her bow.' Does that mean that—"

"Yes, it means that. You and I will be on the *HoYang* to make sure that the yacht and all on board her sinks beneath the waters. Be ready to leave here in an hour. We will gain honor and promotion."

CAREWE WAS LOOKING at some silk shirts in a shop when he felt a tap on the shoulder. He turned to see a man very much like himself in build. But the man's face was hollow-cheeked and lined with the telltale lines of dissipation and his eyes looked as if there were a film over them. Carewe's face was deeply tanned, the skin firm, the lips tight and the eyes clear.

"My sainted Aunt Maria! I say, it's you, Lisle!"

"What's left of me, Carewe. I thought I saw you heading in here. Let's go somewhere we can get a drink. I—I need one badly, old thing."

"Why, of course. Just a second till I get these shirts. I know a giddy place not far from here where we can get good stuff."

After the second drink, Carewe said: "I say, old bean, I don't want you to think I'm asking the jolly old personal question and whatnot, but—are you quite all right? You and I were in the same flaming old squadron and all that sort of rot."

Lisle laughed, a bitter, hard little laugh. "I'm really all right. Thanks for asking, though. Order another round, will you, John?"

"As many as you wish. You know, Bertie, you can't hold me off this way. The Carewes and the Lisles have been too thick for hundreds of years for a Lisle to act upstage with a Carewe way over here in China. When good old Queen Bess was running the show a Lisle saved a Carewe from getting the jolly old bean removed by the headsman's ax and—"

"Oh, damn it all! Stop that. My nerves are shot to hell. I—I—tell me what you are doing. I heard that you were in the north with some Yanks fighting for some kind of swords or whatnot."

"Big Swords."

"That's it. I say, how the mighty have fallen. You fighting for bandits and I am—talk, Carewe. I must get the twitching old nerves under control. You talk and I will drink."

Carewe knew of no reason why he should not talk. He had known Lisle all his life. Known him as a schoolboy, as an officer and a gentleman. He knew Lisle had been dismissed from the service for "conduct unbecoming an officer and a gentleman," but so had other men been dismissed. To him, Lisle was still the chap who fought in the squadron. Carewe had no more hesitancy in talking to him than he would to Jimmie Cordie or Red Dolan.

"The Big Swords are not bandits, old dear. They are mostly Manchus who have good cause to hate the little men of Nippon. An old Manchu noble got them all together and they are called the Big Swords because before we arrived they fought with sword and lance. Jimmie Cordie calls him the Manchu Robin Hood."

Lisle poured out another drink and drank it before he asked: "Isn't this Jimmie Cordie you speak of the chap who fought the machine guns for the war lord of Lingnan down in Cochin-China?"

"Yes," answered Carewe, delighted at getting Lisle interested. "The same Jimmie Cordie. He is a fighting man, Bertie."

"So I have heard. Is he here with you?"

"Yes. We came down to get some guns and ammunition the T'aip'ing got for us."

"The T'aip'ing? You mean the secret society? Are they backing the Big Swords?"

"Well, they are backing Jimmie Cordie, anyway. I don't know about the Big Swords. Jimmie saved the life of the head's only son and since then is their honorable elder brother. Anything he wants, the T'aip'ing get for him."

"I see. Interesting, what? Order another bottle, will you? This one is getting low. So the T'aip'ing got him some guns and ammunition?"

"My hat, I should say they did. A shipload."

"How is he going to get them up in the north? I've heard that the minute one sticks one's nose outside a treaty port it's like no man's land."

"It is. We had to fight our way down. We're going to go up by water as far as the Gulf of Fuchan and then up rivers as far as we can."

"By water?"

"Yes. We are taking the Boston Bean's yacht—or rather, his wife's yacht." Carewe smiled as he thought of the battle Katherine had put up to go along,

"I see. I—look at my hand shake. I wish to—I had gone west in the middle of a dog fight with Fritz."

"Bertie, let me leave you enough of the jolly old filthy to take you out of here somewhere you can—"

"No. I have never allowed any one to—oh, what the hell

is the use of my trying to maintain face? Listen, John, I am shot to pieces more ways than one. Hold everything until I see if I can't get back to what I was for a minute. I—I can't do what—I can't do it, that's all."

"Lisle rides," Carewe said, softly. "Who follows? The leopard banner floats in the wind! Who follows?"

"Stop that! I've stood enough and—Carewe, listen! Get up from this table and go. You hear me? Go. I'll take what's coming to me. For the love of Heaven, Carewe—get out!"

"Not any, old dear. You are unbelted, what, what, what? I am going to see to it that you— I've thought of something. What you need is a sea voyage. We'll take you on the *Katherine* with us and you can come back from where we unload, if you like. If you are feeling fit you can become a Big Sword and—"

"You—you asked me to come on the *Katherine?* Carewe, you asked me, didn't you? I didn't ask you to take me, did I?"

"No, you didn't ask me, Bertie. I asked you. It's all right, old dear. Take another drink and well get going. Plenty of it on board. Have you any clothes? If you haven't we'll stop and get some."

"I have what I stand in, that is all. Carewe, are you sure the rest will not object to your bringing a stranger on board—"

"Object to an old friend of mine who is sick? Your brain must be half drowned in that stuff. Are you quite ready?"

"I'm ready. All things are as Heaven wills, aren't they? There's an old Chinese merchant who's been good to me. I'd like to stop and see him for a minute if you don't mind. If I didn't he might worry about my dropping out of sight."

"We'll stop anywhere you say, old son. A month at sea

will buck you up no end, what, what? You may be a giddy old Big Sword officer yourself before long."

3

THE *KATHERINE* WAS twenty-four hours out of Shanghai, off Shantung in the Yellow Sea. The graceful, white yacht, two hundred and sixty feet long, was slipping easily along through water as still as the water of a mill pond.

The calm, blue-eyed young English captain, who had commanded a mine sweeper in the North Sea during the War and before that sailed the Seven Seas as his forefathers had done since the days of the vikings, was on the bridge. At the wheel, where she loved to be, was Katherine Neville Winthrop.

On the quarterdeck, aft, the Fighting Yid and Red Dolan were stretched lazily out in deck chairs, a table that held bottles and glasses between them.

"This is de life, Irisher," the Yid announced. "Und de von I vos born to. All de Cohens had it yachts bigger dan dis, mit servants to vate upon dem und everything. Mix me a drink und do it mit de snap or I fire it you ven ve get to port."

"What? Me? Mix a drink for the likes of you? A Dolan to mix a drink for a Hester Street bum named—"

Carewe came up and sat down. "I'm not interrupting anything, am I?"

"No," answered the Yid, smirking at Red. "Only dot

Dolan, de Irish low-lifer, vot just gettink started telling me how good de Cohens vos und vot dey did for Ireland."

"Pay no attention to the Yid monkey, Banty. How is your friend by now?"

"Much better, Red. He has got hold of himself. I thought the jolly old salt air would do the trick. He's up on the boat deck taking a walk."

"He was a good man, once. The minute the eyes of me looked at him I could tell that. 'Tis something he has on his mind. That I can also see. Where are the Codfish and George?"

"In the library. Jimmie is taking a nap, I guess. I heard him say something about trying to catch up on some sleep."

"I think I'll take a walk myself. One more second of this Yid and 'tis goofy I'd be. Don't get too near the bum, Carewe, or he'll have your watch."

Both Red and Carewe laughed at the Yid's answer as Red walked away.

Red went to the library where he found the Bean and Grigsby looking at some rare Chinese prints. Red cared nothing for prints, Chinese or otherwise, so after telling the Bean and George what he thought of gentlemen who spent their time looking at "chink paintings" he drifted up on the bridge. There he exchanged gay persiflage with Katherine regarding her steering ability. After that he thought he would follow Jimmie Cordie's example. But once in his cabin he found that he was not at all sleepy. At last he decided to go up to the wireless room and swap a few lies with Murphy, the operator.

As he opened the door of the wireless room he saw

Murphy stretched out on the floor and Lisle rising from the chair at the desk.

Red had no more reason to be suspicious of Lisle than Carewe had, but the years he had put in as lieutenant of military police—much to his disgust, he wanting to be at the front with Jimmie Cordie or the Bean—had given him a sort of sixth sense. He knew, in a split second, that Lisle was an enemy.

"What happened to Murphy?" he demanded, advancing into the room.

"Why—I don't know, Dolan. I came in a minute ago and saw him there on the floor. I—"

"You saw him on the floor and sat down at his desk. How long ago was that?"

"My word! I arrived just a second before you did, old dear. I sat down to see if there was something wrong. Something that could have given him an electric shock."

"You are a damn liar. You were sending a message to some one. Who were you sending it to? Come clean with me before I slap your nose around behind the ears."

"Before you what? You must be drunk or—"

Murphy sat up, feeling the back of his neck. "What the hell hit me? Was it you, Dolan? Wait till I get on my feet, you big red-headed bum. I'll learn you to hit a Murphy from behind."

" 'Twas not me that hit you. Stand where you are, Lisle. What happened, Murphy?"

"How do I know? I was sitting there doing nothing when I heard some one come in. I started to turn my head and something hit me on the back of the neck. That's all I know until I woke up and saw you standing there."

"He must have had some kind of a shock and fallen from his chair," Lisle said.

"Bushwah! Why did you sneak up behind Murphy and hit him? What did you use, a blackjack?"

"Oh, I say, this has gone quite too far, you know. Stand to one side, Dolan. I am Carewe's guest and I do not want to have to use force." As he spoke he took a step forward.

Red's right hand came against Lisle's chest and pushed him back. "I told you to stay put. Do it and you won't get hurt. Murphy, get up from that floor and go and get Jimmie Cordie. 'Tis he that will—"

LISLE, HIS NERVES taut, thinking of many things that exposure would mean, lost his head. It came to him that he could fight his way past Red, get a life belt and go overboard. Better that, with the chance he could win to shore, than stay and face Carewe.

He crouched and sprang at Red's throat. In Japan he had been taught many jujutsu holds. The real ones—not those taught to people who wish to learn out of curiosity. One of them he had applied to Murphy's neck. A hold that instantly puts a man out for a few minutes. Now, as he closed with Red, he was going to use a hold that kills.

But Red knew holds, too. Not jujutsu holds but holds learned in the Foreign Legion, where there are, as the Yid once said, "a lot of di-ert-ty fighters," when they find it necessary to meet fire with fire. And some of the Battalion of Africa—to which men of the French service are sent when they are too tough even for the legion—had shown Red, whom they liked, some of their tricks. Also, Red was a graduate of the street fighting in Dublin and Cork.

The Irish are not noted for caring much about rules

while engaged in rough-and-tumble fighting and Red was known as a good man to keep away from in a fight.

Lisle's charge was that of a lean, mad wolverine. Red's defense was that of an angry grizzly bear. His hands slapped the outstretched hands of Lisle far apart. So far that they were three feet from Red's body when Red brought his right knee up. Lisle snarled like a wounded animal and swerved to one side. Then in at Red again, to be met and hurled back. In again and this time Red picked him up and flung him against the wall, but before he did it, Lisle hurt him badly. The Englishman bounced to his feet as a rubber ball bounces from the floor and literally flung himself at Red.

Murphy, on his feet and back against the wall near the door, muttered: "For the love of Heaven, what kind of fighting is that?" He had never seen a fight like it and he had seen, and been, in plenty.

It was a nasty thing to watch. Lisle's head had been cut when he hit the wall and he was bleeding, as Murphy described it later, "like a stuck pig." Red met him once with a straight right to nose and mouth and there wasn't much left of nose or mouth but a bloody smear. Red's left arm had been snapped like a pipe stem by a hold Lisle had made stick for a moment and his right side felt as if some one were holding a red-hot poker against it.

There seemed to be no stopping Lisle. He fought with the savagery of a man gone amok. The slim, boyish English-man carried the fight to Red Dolan, something few men ever did after the first two or three minutes.

Once Red was off balance and Lisle brought him down,

falling with him. They worried each other like a couple of wild cats.

At last, Red threw Lisle off, got up, stooped, picked Lisle up and then slammed him down on the floor.

Murphy said: "Oh, my Lord! You've killed—"

Red turned and looked at him. "Didn't I tell you to go and get Jimmie? Do it or I'll—I'll—" He swayed forward, caught himself, came erect, swayed again and this time went to the floor himself and stayed there. Lisle lay still, a broken thing that had once been a man.

4

JIMMIE CORDIE, GRIGSBY and the Fighting Yid stood on one side of a cot in the yacht's sick bay. On the other side Carewe stood with the ship's doctor. There was another cot in the sick bay, occupied by Red Dolan, who was sitting up. Katherine sat on the edge of Red's cot, near the foot. Red's arm had been set and he had been relieved of various aches and pains. The doctor was looking down at Lisle.

"I shot the dope into him because I could not half fix him up while he was under the ether. I didn't dare to keep him under longer on account of his heart. It's fifty fifty whether he ever wakes up or not. If he does, let Carewe speak to him first, if he's sane. There is about one chance in a million that he will be and—he's coming out. Get so he can see you, Carewe, when he opens his eyes."

Lisle opened his eyes and tried to sit up but could not make it. He fell back. "That you, Carewe? Is—it time to—go up and hunt for Fritzie? My word—what a—a dream I had. I feel all smashed up."

"Steady. You've been hurt, old chap. Tell me who you are with and what—"

"Who I am with? I don't know what you—what you—is it you, John? The Yanks don't matter, do they? I didn't know that a Neville was—was—is there a Neville here? I—what difference does anything make? Move out—I want to go back to—sleep."

The doctor shook his head and as he did Katherine stepped to the foot of Lisle's cot. "The leopard of the Lisle has turned into a jackal," she said, coldly and distinctly.

Lisle raised himself on an elbow, eyes wide open. It was as if the words had tapped a reserve of strength in his body. "Who said that?"

"I said it," Katherine answered, her voice as cold as northern ice in the gray dawn. "I said it. I, a Neville. The pied bull of Neville has fought many a stricken field, side by side with the leopard of Lisle and they were both there at the end, come weal or woe. The bull was proud to be at the side of the leopard but now—the leopard of Lisle has turned into a jackal. A jackal that permits a woman of the Neville to go into unseen danger—because the jackal is afraid of something."

Lisle was staring at her daring her speech, seeing no one else in the room. After she finished he said: "You—a Neville—say that to a Lisle? Know that— Oh, my Lord! I remember now. I—the leopard warns the pied bull. Look out for the *Ho*—" He fell back, dead before his head touched the pillow.

"It was a good try, Katherine," Jimmie Cordie said, gently. "Let's go somewhere and see if we can dope this thing out."

"Two of you carry this damn cot," Red demanded. "Don't be leaving me here, Jimmie darling. I'm all right."

"I'll pack one end of it. Yid, take the other. Far be it from me to leave you anywhere, Mr. Dolan."

On the way to the library, Red asked: "Jimmie, what is a pied bull? Did herself mean the bull was pie-eyed drunk?"

"No, Red," Jimmie answered, gravely, as he always did when Red asked for information. "A pied bull means a bull that is mottled."

"Mottled? An' what the hell is mottled?"

"That means that the bull is of two or three colors. A white-and-black bull is a mottled or pied bull, as I understand it. So is a black-and-white-and-brown one—or a sky-blue-pink-and-yellow one. Like a horse they called a calico, sabe?"

"I do. The hide is of different colors. What is herself doing with a pied bull?"

"The banner of the Nevilles is a pied bull on a white background. Same as the Dolan banner is a shillalah held in the right hand of a red-headed ape."

"If my good left arm was well, you wouldn't be saying that, you small-sized shrimp of the world."

"Says you, that's all. Shut up or we'll drop you."

IN THE LIBRARY, after Red was placed on a couch and propped up by cushions, he having insisted on getting off the cot, Jimmie said: "Carewe, tell us about Lisle. First, let me say—and I know I say it for all of us—that we know you are all wool and a yard wide. Whatever happens, the only thing you had to do with it is that you were taken for a nice buggy ride."

"Thank you, Jimmie. It looks very much as if I had been taken for a buggy ride—whatever that is. I can't realize that a Lisle could sink so low as to—"

"Speaking of sinking, let it go at that. We may all be sunk pronto unless we dope it out. Tell us about Lisle."

THEY LISTENED WITHOUT interruption while Carewe told them how Lisle picked him up.

Then Jimmie Cordie said: "The only people who are interested in stopping the Big Swords from getting guns and ammunition are the Japs. You say he tried to put jujutsu holds on you, Red?"

"Tried? Tried, is it? He did put them on me. Do you think he broke the arm of me by kissing it? But, thanks be to the good saints above, I had some myself that broke most of his."

"Jimmie," Katherine said, "do you think he was sending to a Japanese war-ship?"

"Well—I don't think so, Katherine. No Jap warship would dare fire on a ship of a friendly—by gosh, he meant the *HoYang!*"

"And what the heck is the *HoYang?*" demanded Red.

"The *HoYang*, Mr. Dolan, is the flagship of a pirate gent named Ying-chau. He has been running high, wide and handsome in these here waters for a year or more. I guess he thinks he is king of all pirates. Instead of flying the skull and crossbones he flies his own flag and—"

"How come you know all about him? Did you sail mit?"

"No, my fair Hester Street friend, I did not sail mit. I have my own pirate fleet. All kidding aside, I know it because not long ago he sank two T'aip'ing junks and right now the T'aip'ing war fleet is looking for Mr. Ying-chau. My guess is that Lisle was hooked up with Ying-chau and—that's not so good. If he was—where do the Japs come in?"

"Maybeso dey ain't in. Vot do ve care who is in und who ain't? Dis guy wires it to some von dot ve are heading for so und so in dus und such a position, don't he? Den dey know vare to be ven ve come along. Poppa vill dope it oud for de kiddies."

"Yeah? Well—poppa is some doper out, at that. Did you tell him at any time that we were going up the river Kiang-Lu?"

"Why—I may have mentioned it, Jimmie. Remember we all talked about things at the dinner table last night."

"That's right, we did. No use fussing about the whys and wherefores. We are going to be met by some one to whom Lisle wirelessed."

"But," the Bean said, "how did he know he could get to the wireless, and at that, why go to all the trouble? We were spotted in Shanghai and why couldn't a Jap destroyer or this *HoYang* get us right after we left? Why all this—"

"Your guess is as good as mine. Maybe we are faster and also maybe they did not want to take us over until we reached the open sea where there would be no witnesses. All we know is that it is a cinch some one is laying for us—somewhere."

"Why all the wah-wah? Let's be getting ready for the black-hearted devil, whoever he is."

"Those are words of wisdom, Mr. Dolan," the Bean answered. "But there is very little getting ready needed once we are assured that the bugler knows where his bugle is. Maybe we can find you a sword. I know Jeems has his .45 along. I saw her."

"Vot could be sveeter?" the Yid asked. "Jimmie mit a gat und de Irish bummer mit a sword. Poppa vill go und take it a nap."

They all laughed, save Carewe. He could not, thinking of Lisle.

"Jimmie, did you say that this pirate flies his own flag?"

"Yes. Mrs. Beaneater. He thinks his flag scares 'em more than the regular pirate flag. Why?"

"Why—nothing. Only—if we are to engage him I think that I will—I brought one to give to John and I am sure it is in my trunk. John said once that he would like to have one, so I— It's just something I was thinking of, Jimmie."

"We all understand you very fully," the Bean said, gravely. "You need not explain further."

Katherine wrinkled her pretty nose at them as the reckless soldiers of fortune laughed, then said: "Come on, Carewe. Come and help me do something. We'll leave these—these darned old Yanks to themselves."

5

THE *HOYANG LAY* off the Gulf of Pechili into which the river Kiang-Lu empties. Her engines were turning over just enough to give her seaway.

She was a big ship, as Chinese freighters go, some two hundred feet long and thirty-odd feet from her boat deck to the water line.

On her bridge stood Ying-chau, her captain, Major Tota, Captain Yatsu and the sailor at the wheel.

"She ought to be coming in sight very soon," Major Tota said, as he looked at his watch. "The message was not at all definite and broke off suddenly."

"I hope what you did get was correct," Captain Yatsu answered, hiding a yawn. He did not care at all for this being on a Chinese pirate ship and keeping awake at what to him were ungodly hours.

"It is correct," Major Tota said, grimly. "He knows what would happen to him if he gave me incorrect information."

"You said once that—what was it? That he would hang in Nippon?"

"Yes. He was cashiered from the British army because of some trouble with a woman—rather, over a woman. She was the wife of a staff officer and so—it is a long story, captain. While we are waiting for the Katherine I will tell you some of it.

"At last he reached Nippon. He was by then what the English call a bum. And to be a foreign bum in Nippon is not at all pleasant, I imagine. He robbed and when resistance was offered, killed another Englishman who was traveling in Kiushu, my province. While awaiting his trail, I talked to him several times and—one night he escaped. Do you understand?"

"Yes, major. And since his escape he has done as you ordered."

"Exactly. And he still does. In talking about the Big Sword mongrels he said that he knew Carewe."

"I should think, as an Englishman, he would much rather be hanged. Or die by his own hand."

"Why? There was nothing concerning England in what I have required of him up to date. Now there is only one Englishman and one Englishwoman concerned in the matter. Englishmen have killed Englishmen before now, captain, and no doubt Englishwomen also. He himself killed one to rob him. As far as dying by his own hand, it seems, as he told me, the code of his clan or house does not permit it. They must fight on to their last breath."

"I see. How are you going to save him from the *Katherine?*"

"I ordered him to go over the side when the guns open. If he can make it to the *HoYang* he will be picked up. Frankly, I do not care whether he does or not. His habits are gaining on him and soon he will be of no further use to us."

"If he were picked up, he would know that we— There is a ship!"

Major Tota brought out his glasses. "It is the *Katherine.* Run up the distress signal, Captain Ying-chau."

Two small flags went up, one—the highest—a blue-and-white check, the other—below the first—a white flag with a large red dot close to the wide end. They were international commercial code flags, meaning, "In distress. Want immediate assistance."

Ten minutes later Major Tota announced: "She is coming. Soon we will be avenged on the curs who thought they could flout the intelligence of Nippon. They will be food for the fish inside of an hour. It looks as if she would come on the port side, Captain Ying-chau."

"It makes no difference, mighty one. Either port or starboard, we have her. The machine guns will sweep her bridge and she will be out of control. Then we will open up and sink her. She is close enough now for me to— I crave permission to run up my flag."

"You have it. Captain Yatsu. We will go below and watch from a port-hole."

As the two Japanese officers left the bridge, another flag was run up. This flag had a single Chinese character on it, meaning "snake" or "a poisonous snake."

"She comes bow on," the pirate captain said to one of his officers who had come on the bridge. He was puzzled. "She must see my flag by now and—there goes a flag up. It is not the flag of England or of America. See, she swings now to port and—she comes across our bow! Open fire! Open fire!"

THE *KATHERINE*, WITHIN one thousand yards, had swung just a little to port, as if to come up on the starboard side of the *HoYang*, and then turned to starboard. The graceful, white yacht seemed to leap through the water as it started to cross the bow of the *HoYang*. And as she did, the banner of the Neville straightened out in the breeze from the *Katherine's* steel military mast.

The *HoYang* opened fire with machine guns and immediately two four-inch rifles spoke. The machine guns swept the bridge of the *Katherine*. Three figures fell. But, to the amazement of the pirates, the *Katherine* kept right on her course.

The figures were dummies, the *Katherine* being steered and fought from a conning tower of chilled steel plate, camouflaged as a smoke stack. That is about all most of the pirates on the deck of the *HoYang* ever saw on this earth. It may be that they saw flame leap from gun muzzles.

The deck houses of the *Katherine* dropped sides and guns appeared. All along her side, ports opened and the lean, brown muzzles of heavy guns slid out.

A deadly sleet of steel rained on the *HoYang* from stem to stern, bringing death to all on her bridge and deck. One of the four-inch shells from the *HoYang* went over the *Katherine*, the other tore a hole in her bow above the water line.

"Port," commanded Katherine Neville Winthrop, coldly. She was in the conning tower with the English captain who was conning the yacht—under her orders. He smiled, knowing that the obeyed order would take the *Katherine* in close to the *HoYang*—and they did not know what she carried beside the two four-inch rifles. But he brought the *Katherine* to port as if she were a rowboat, and went in with her.

As she passed the *HoYang* she sent shell after shell into the Chinese ship. Rapid fire and machine guns raked the *HoYang* with a fire that was deadly in its accuracy. The yacht went the entire length without receiving a return fire. The pirate gunners on that side of the *HoYang*, on the four-inch guns, had been killed by a shell that exploded right over the guns.

As the *Katherine* flashed by, every gun that could be was brought to bear in commission. Major Tota and Captain Yatsu lay flat on the deck below. They knew that instead of trapping, the *HoYang* had been trapped.

As the *Katherine's* stem passed the stern of the *HoYang*, the Neville ordered: "Take her to the starboard side of this pirate who flies a flag of his own."

"How close, Mrs. Winthrop?" asked the captain, calmly.

"Alongside. We will board her, captain. I will lesson this Chinese dog in regard to firing on the Neville banner."

As he turned the yacht, the captain thought of the story about the Neville and the great Spanish Armada. He thought that the dainty girl beside him was most certainly a throwback to that Neville. And she was, at that—at least when it came to fighting.

As the yacht came alongside, the *HoYang* fired the guns on that side. This time the *Katherine* was hit twice amidships. But the shells exploded between decks, missing the engine gun.

The library, the dining saloon and the galley were knocked into a cocked hat, two guns put out of commission and a fire started, which was promptly put out.

The *Katherine* answered the fire, gun muzzles almost touching the *HoYang*, the fire directed at the open gun ports. When she rubbed sides with the ship there were no gun muzzles sticking out of the *HoYang* to hold her off. They had been blown from their carriages and hurled back.

The crew of the *Katherine,* all American and English veterans, passed the word as she closed in. "Hot damn! We are going to take her by hand. Get ready, you guys!" They got ready, with bayoneted rifles and .45 revolvers.

As the yacht touched the *HoYang,* Katherine came out of the conning tower. "Boarders away! We take this pirate dog!"

She fully intended to lead the boarding party. But she did not. The Boston Bean had expected something like that and was ready for her. As Katherine took a step forward he came around with two of the crew. Without a word he picked the fighting Neville up in his arms and tossed her at Red, who caught her with his right arm. "Take care of her, you redheaded ape," he shouted as he ran to join the boarding party, already at the rail.

Jimmie Cordie laughed. "That's the boy, Codfish! Come on, you roughnecks! Show me something!"

And as he leaped down to the *HoYang's* deck, every man of the crew that could leave his battle station came on. The chief engineer, armed with a thirty-six-inch spanner, walked side by side with the doctor, who had an automatic riot shotgun.

The chief, whose name was MacAleney, had said to his second: "Listen, you! I am going up. See to it thot you stick ar-r-r-r-ound wid me engines or-r-r-r I'll take this wee fist and I'll push the nose ave you ar-r-r-ound back of them big ears."

What the second said when MacAleney was out of hearing would not be printed. He wanted "up" himself.

THE PIRATES—WHAT WAS left of them—on the *HoYang* fought viciously. But here were no cringing junk or steamer crew to slay. Here were big, lean men with bayoneted rifles and heavy revolvers, who fought with little frozen smiles on their lips and in their eyes. Men who contemptuously parried a sword cut with a rifle barrel and then drove a bayonet home. Men who answered a poorly aimed shot with a well-aimed one.

From deck to deck and from bow to stern, the veterans of the *Katherine* hunted the pirates as terriers hunt rats.

Jimmie Cordie and the Fighting Yid ran along a line of cabins, opening or breaking the doors. In one of them Major Tota and Captain Yatsu had taken refuge. As the two Japanese went into the cabin, Major Tota said: "They have taken the *HoYang*. We are prisoners of the pirates. Play up promptly, Captain Yatsu."

Not long afterward the door crashed open and Jimmie Cordie entered, his .45 held near his hip.

"Do not shoot," Major Tota said, calmly. "We are Japanese officers held prisoner by the pirate curs. I am Major Tota and this is Captain Yatsu."

"All right. Stay put for a few minutes. Yid, stay with them."

"Oi, I vant to—"

"Go right ahead. I'll stay."

"Vot? I vill stay, Jimmie. I vos only kidding."

"Yeah? Do your kidding some other time."

It was half an hour before Jimmie Cordie came back to the cabin. "Let's go. Get in front, Yid. Walk between us, gentlemen."

"We wish to thank you for rescuing us from—"

"Later, major. The *HoYang* is sinking."

One of the crew of the *Katherine* ran up. "Captain

Cordie, Mike Egan and that damn engineer are still hunting chinks and won't pay any attention to the order to come up."

"I'll get 'em. Go ahead, Yid. Take the gentlemen to the *Katherine*. Go with Captain Cohen, Tommy."

The Yid stalked ahead of the two Japanese. He was more or less peeved because he had lost out on some of the hunting. The Yid always wanted to be in the thick of things. There were dead and wounded pirates scattered all around the decks. As his party neared a place that looked as if a machine gun had registered full on, a wounded Chinese staggered to his feet. He was a ghastly sight, looking like a bloody, torn caricature of a man. The pirate was Yingchau's brother and had been second in command. In his right hand he held a straight, short sword.

"You dogs," he snarled in Chinese, blood running from between his lips. "You Nippon dogs! You would trap the foreign devils, would you? And now—they have trapped us and we all die. We die and you still live? I will—" The sword flew as an arrow flies, to and through the heart of Major Tota.

As the sword flashed through the air, the Yid stepped to one side and raised his gun. Captain Yatsu's hand went under his blouse and came out with a Japanese service revolver in it. He shot once, hitting the already falling pirate between the eyes.

"Drop dot gat," the Yid commanded. The Yid understood very little Chinese, but he knew enough to understand that the Jap was getting bawled out for the failure of something.

To give the Japanese due credit, they are fearless as far

as physical courage is concerned. Captain Yatsu was no exception. He thought that the Yid had understood all of what the Chinese said and it may be he also thought that if he surrendered he would get the same treatment the soldiers of fortune would have received at the hands of the Japanese.

Whatever he thought, he did not drop his gun. He started to swing it into line with the Yid. It had not traveled more than an inch before a bullet from the Yid's .45 crashed between his eyes and he fell beside Major Tota, dead before his body hit the deck.

"Vot de hell vos dot guy thinking of?" demanded the Yid. "My gat vos on him und—"

"What came off?" Jimmie Cordie asked as he came up with several of the crew.

"Vell, most of de top of de midget's head, for von thing. I said. 'Drop de gat,' und I had mine full on him. He didn't did it und so—"

"I saw all that. What happened, before?"

"Von of dese chinks gets up und bawls dem out in chink talk for diding something. Den he—"

The *HoYang* gave a sickening, slow lurch to port, righted herself and then lurched again. This time she did not come back to even keel.

Jimmie Cordie laughed. "Tell me the rest some other time. All hands on deck!"

THE CREW OF the **Katherine,** Jimmie Cordie and the Yid, made it back to the yacht by, as the Yid said later, "De skin of de vell-known teeth, ain't it?"

The dead and wounded of the crew were already on board and the *Katherine* drew away from the *HoYang*.

Three minutes later, the pirate craft owned by the Japanese intelligence went down, carrying with her the dead and wounded. As she went, the Boston Bean quoted gravely, watching her from the bridge of the *Katherine*. "Those that live by the sword, die by the sword. Is that quoted right, Jeems?"

"I don't know, Codfish," Jimmie Cordie answered. "And I guess it doesn't make much difference to the gentlemen who manned the *HoYang* whether it is or not. Do your quoting some other time. Let's see where we stand."

COLONEL NAGAYA, JAPANESE military intelligence, sat at his desk, staring down at a message held in his right hand, which, in spite of his efforts, shook a little.

The message read:

> To Japanese Military Intelligence, Harbin. This, to inform you that Major Tota and Captain Yatsu, Japanese officers, who were on board the pirate ship *HoYang*, were both killed during the action that sunk her.

It was signed: "Captain James Cordie, Chief of Staff, The Big Swords."

www.ingramcontent.com/pod-product-compliance
Lightning Source LLC
Chambersburg PA
CBHW030533030726
47495CB00004B/978